"Honey, didn't you hear?" Dad's brown eyes smiled, but his arm tightened around me. "Marcie and I—w-we're..."

"We're going to be married!" Marcie finished triumphantly.

"I...I don't believe..." Waves of shock sucked my words.

Amy hurtled over to my dad, her yellow pigtails bobbing. "Yay! Can you be my daddy now?"

The log in the fire shifted with a thud, sending a spray of sparks onto the rug. I jumped up and stamped out the tiny glows. "I don't believe it! I don't believe it!" I said with each kick.

Marcie went on. "We're planning a July wedding as soon as your graduation is over, Sunday. I hope that's okay with you."

Okay? I wanted to kill her. Her marrying my dad? Nothing could be less okay in the world!

# It's A TERRIBLE Age To Be

### BY JANA NOVOTNY HUNTER

Photo by John Strange

Published by Worthington Press
7099 Huntley Road, Worthington, Ohio 43085

Printed in the United States of America
10 9 8 7 6 5 4 3 2 1

ISBN 0-87406-388-4

*For Richard*

# *One*

I hate to share.

I knew it way back in preschool when this kid named Susu wanted my teddy bear. I'd brought my teddy bear in for show-and-tell, and Susu tried to grab him from me. We both pulled and yanked at him, yelling like crazy until...Bingo! He split in two.

Susu got his head and body.

I got one mangled arm.

That's what you get for sharing.

I rest my case.

I don't go to preschool anymore. I'm about to graduate from Luther Junior High, but I feel the same way about sharing as I did back then.

Take today at school when I forgot my lunch. My friend Julie said I could share hers. Knowing how much she loves to eat, I appreciated the thought, but I said no. Why should

I force my best friend to share?

Julie has been my best friend since grade school when she told me that my name was different but pretty. My name is Sunday Moon Fairchild. She looked the same now as she did back then—small, dark, and plump. The only difference is that she wears braces now.

She closed her mouth down over the braces and threw up her short arms. "Sunday Moon, I can't believe that you'd rather eat the school's food than share my lunch."

I looked at her and shrugged. "I'd rather eat the school's food than share." I grinned. "You know I'm a spoiled-rotten, only child."

"That's about the only good thing about being Carl's sister—it has taught me to put up with anything."

"I'll say."

Outwardly, Julie and I are total opposites. I am tall and thin, with long, straight, blond hair. Julie is short and stocky and has dark, curly hair. I have gray eyes, and Julie has brown eyes. But even though we look different, we think the same way most of the time.

I get my looks from my mother, my dad says. She died when I was a baby. I have a picture of my mom, and I sure hope I've inherited her figure.

"Do you know what I hate sharing the most?" I asked Julie as we pushed our way through the crowds to get to the cafeteria.

"What?"

"I hate sharing my dad with Marcie."

Julie frowned. "It's weird for your dad to have a girlfriend. He's never had one before."

"The only girlfriend he's ever had was my mom." I pushed hard on the doors of the cafeteria. "Why did he have to meet Marcie? I can't wait for them to break up."

Julie didn't bother to answer. With all the noise in the cafeteria, I wouldn't have heard her, anyway.

"Get us seats," I mouthed to her.

The cafeteria smelled like overcooked hamburger and boiled sneakers. It always smelled that way, whether the menu was shrunken hot dogs or flaky fish sticks. It was really weird how students pushed through the lines, like they couldn't wait to eat that junk. One skinny kid with stick-out hair and elbows almost knocked me down.

I picked out a tuna fish sandwich, a limp salad, and a carton of juice and yelled, "Excuse me! Can I get through?"

By some miracle, Julie had managed to get two seats together. I barreled my way through the crowds to her. She was unpacking her lunch. Nothing comes between Julie and her food—natural disasters, fathers dating witches—they all wilt in comparison to a double-decker salami on rye.

I flopped down and snapped open my carton of juice. "I can't wait for them to break up," I murmured again. "After all, Marcie Vane is not Dad's type."

Julie set out her cupcake, fruit punch, and yogurt in a row. "Maybe his type has changed. Your dad is surprising you a lot lately."

I sighed. "That's true. After a lifetime of honesty, he dates Miss Phoney of the Year." I prodded my lettuce. "She acts like she's one of the models instead of the dumb photographer."

Julie chewed on her sandwich. "She sure looks like a model. She's so tall and skinny..."

I interrupted before she could go any further. "I wish Dad had never written that piece on L.A. Fashions. Since he met Marcie, he goes around humming Beatles music all day.

"It sounds like he's in love," Julie said.

"Don't even think it." I tore at my bread, wishing it was Marcie's hair I was pulling. "On top of that, she has to come over tonight. Fridays are always my time with Dad—*alone*."

"Maybe they're going to break it to you that

they're getting married."

"No way."

"So, why do you think your dad's planning this big dinner?" Julie asked. "And why is Marcie bringing over her kid?"

"Do you mean Amy? I don't know..." My insides felt funny all of a sudden. If Julie were right and my dad was thinking about marrying Marcie, I was in for some major sharing. Suddenly, it felt like I'd eaten a whole plateful of those boiled sneakers.

*Julie must be wrong. Dad promised me that he'd never get married again after losing Mom.* We Fairchilds are famous for keeping our word. That's why I was so upset with Dad. He'd never exactly promised not to date, but it was understood. Now I was confused. *Why couldn't it always be Dad and me without a dumb girlfriend like Marcie?*

I had started to wonder if Dad was getting serious with Marcie. He had certainly hinted about it enough, talking about "new beginnings" and how the pain of losing Mom was finally healed. I worried about it all afternoon. I even messed up in music. I couldn't get the opening notes of the solo flute piece I was practicing for graduation.

I talked to Julie about it when we walked home from school in the California sun. "I had my solo down perfectly last night. Today I was awful. See what all this worrying is doing to me?"

"I know. Look," Julie touched my arm gently, "I'm probably wrong about your dad."

I smiled gratefully at her. "I hope so. What beats me is why Marcie would like someone who wears old T-shirts and jeans instead of designer clothes. With her fashion sense, you'd think she'd go for someone cool."

"Maybe she's changed. Marcie sure has changed your dad."

"Don't say that." I didn't like to admit it, but Dad had changed. Lately he was trimming his beard and ironing his shirts. He was even relaxed when he was working at his typewriter.

"Okay. I won't say another word."

"I know you're trying to help, Jule. But Dad will never be like Marcie." I stared down the long, tree-lined avenue ahead. "He doesn't go for status symbols."

"Like Marcie's white Porsche?"

"Right. I think she even polishes the tires."

Julie laughed. "I can't imagine Marcie getting her hands dirty."

"Valet service, my dear," I said, mimicking an upper-class drawl. "Or maybe she gets her housekeeper, Winnie, to do it."

We turned into Julie's driveway. Julie's

house is like our house, only bigger. It's a long, California ranch house with redwood siding. Julie leaned against the creaky fence around her house and sighed. "Look, I have to go. I have a painting class at the art center. Let me know what happens tonight, okay?"

"If you don't hear from me, you'll know that you were right and that I've become a runaway statistic," I said mournfully.

Slowly, I walked the two blocks to my house. It was quiet, except for a couple of kids on their bikes. The town I live in, Tarzana, is pretty small, but I really like living there. It's a quiet town, even though Los Angeles is only 30 miles away. And who else can claim that they live in a place named after Tarzan?

The house was empty. It looked like Dad had a cleaning binge without me. The whole place smelled like disinfectant. The sofa had been cleared of papers, and my flute music had been stacked in neat piles on the coffee table. Everything in the kitchen had been scoured until it shone. Even the countertops had been cleared.

I saw one of Dad's rhyming notes on the refrigerator.

*Friday 3:30 p.m.*

*Sunday Mouse,*

*Tonight is Open House!*

*We're in for some fun!*
*Gone to pick up dessert from Mischa's.*
*Won't it taste great after my special pizzas?*

*Love, Dad*
*P.S. Do your flute first (I know you think I am the worst!)*

Mischa's makes the best desserts in town. We only have them on important occasions like birthdays or when Dad finishes a big assignment. Did his getting dessert there mean that tonight was a special occasion?

By the time Marcie and Amy arrived, I was close to panic. I dropped everything and knocked into furniture like a complete klutz. And for the first time that I can remember, I didn't enjoy Dad's homemade pizza. It stuck in my throat.

I kept catching Dad and Marcie giving each other long, meaningful looks.

I timed them. One lasted 10 whole seconds. And as if that wasn't bad enough, I had to sit across from Amy, Marcie's four-year-old daughter. Little kids are okay, but this one is the pits. Kids who look innocent with long, blond hair and blue eyes don't fool me.

Last week, Marcie had the nerve to say that we could be sisters because of our coloring. I immediately pointed out that my eyes are not blue. They are gray.

Tonight, as I watched Amy sitting next to my dad at the table, I practiced making my eyes into slits like a cat's eyes.

No one noticed. They were too busy watching Amy as she created a scene.

"How come I don't get any?" she yelled, jiggling up and down when dad took the dessert out of the refrigerator.

"You're next, honey," Marcie said softly.

But that didn't satisfy the brat. As soon as she got hers, she whined, "Sunday's is bigger than mine!"

Marcie whispered in the syrupy voice she always uses when she talks to Amy, "Eat that first. Then you can have some more."

*I hope it makes you sick,* I thought, making my eyes slices of gray.

I felt like throwing up as I watched Amy feed her toy owl with real food. The owl had gook matted all the way down its front. She takes that terrible toy owl everywhere—even to the bathroom. It's ridiculous.

When dessert was over, Dad got up.

"Why don't we have coffee in the den?" he suggested, pretending to be casual. "The evening's chilly, so Sunday built a fire."

He forgot to mention that he had *told* me to do it.

Sitting on the rug in front of the fire, I studied the flames. I wanted to keep my back to the room and blot out the sound of Marcie's voice. The crackling logs reminded me of the times Dad and I would turn out the lights and listen to *Mystery Theater* in the firelight.

"Sunday, are you listening?" Dad asked, interrupting my thoughts. "This is important." He came and sat beside me, circling my shoulders with his arm.

"Mmm? Oh, I'm sorry." I turned around to see Marcie still talking.

"Joe and I thought it was the right time to tell you..." Marcie was saying.

"Tell us? Tell us what?"

"Honey, didn't you hear?" Dad's brown eyes smiled, but his arm tightened. "Marcie and I—we—we're—"

"We're going to be married!" Marcie finished triumphantly.

"I—I don't believe..." I stammered, as waves of shock sucked away my words.

Amy hurtled over to my dad, her yellow pigtails bobbing. "Yay! Can you be my daddy now?"

The log in the fire shifted with a thud, sending a spray of sparks onto the rug. I jumped up and stamped out the tiny glows. "I don't believe it! I don't believe it!" I said with each kick.

But Marcie just went on. "We're planning a July wedding, as soon as your graduation is over, Sunday. I hope that's okay with you."

*Okay?* I wanted to kill her. Her marrying my dad!? Nothing could be less okay in the world.

"Sunday, what do you think?" asked Dad. He came up behind me and stroked the back of my head.

I spun around to face him. I didn't say a word. He wouldn't want to know what I thought.

His lined face looked as confused as I felt. But I could see hope written all over it, pleading with me.

Amy bounced around. "Can I be a bridesmaid?"

I dragged my eyes from Dad's face and looked at the two people who were ruining my life.

Marcie gave Amy her lipstick-smeared

smile. "Of course, you can. You and Sunday are going to be twin bridesmaids."

"That's what you think," I muttered.

Marcie leaned over to Amy and stroked her cheek. "Sunday can stay with you Amy, honey, when Mommy and your new daddy take our honeymoon cruise."

I squeaked at Dad, "Honeymoon?" My voice got louder. "What do you mean, *honeymoon?*"

"Well, Sunday," Dad nervously stroked his beard. "That's the other thing we wanted to talk to you about."

"Talk? Talk?" I yelled. "Count me out of your talk!"

Marcie, Amy, and even Dad's trusting face blurred as the tears streamed from my eyes. I ran out of the room sobbing.

This was the worst day of my life.

# Two

I cried most of the night. A couple of times Dad came up and knocked on the door, but I told him to go away. Finally I heard him sigh and say that we'd "talk about it" in the morning. *Talk.* What he meant was *listen.* He sure wouldn't want to hear what I had to say.

I was playing a sad piece on my flute the next morning when he knocked on my bedroom door.

"Sunday, please get dressed and come down to breakfast."

*Who could eat?* I thought.

"Okay." I slid off my bed and went downstairs.

The kitchen looked normal. It was sunny and bright, as if the major bomb of the century had not been dropped.

Dad had prepared all my favorite things—pancakes with syrup, fresh strawberries, and whipped cream.

"Sunday, I know this isn't easy for you, but please try to understand. It means so much to me."

"I know," I said, helping myself to some pancakes.

"I don't expect you to like the idea, but in time..." he continued.

I stabbed at a strawberry. "You said that you would never marry again."

"And I meant it when I said it. I thought I would never love anyone the way I loved your mother. But Marcie is different."

"I'll say," I muttered under my breath.

"She understands me, Sunday. It's like she's put together the pieces that were missing since I lost your mother. She...she's made me feel whole again."

"I haven't been unhappy these last years," Dad went on, as if speaking to himself. "It's been wonderful, just watching you grow up into a beautiful, young woman. But a part of me that I thought was dead has come back since I met Marcie."

I stared out the window at the ivy on our backyard wall, embarrassed. I didn't know what to say.

"Marcie is a really nice person when you get to know her, Sunday. She wants to be your friend. So does Amy."

"I'll pick my own friends."

"I think you'll grow to like Marcie and Amy if you give them a chance," Dad said lightly.

I knew I'd hurt him just then. "I'm sorry, Dad."

"Just try. That's all I ask. Just try."

I crammed a huge piece of pancake into my mouth so I wouldn't have to speak. Even I knew that if you have to try to like someone it never works.

Dad moved his large hand across the table and covered mine.

"Sunday, I love you. But I have to plan a future of my own. You're growing up so fast. What am I going to do when you run off to be a concert flutist?"

It was true. I wasn't a kid anymore. I looked at him. "What about my graduation?"

"What do you mean?"

"Will *they* have to come?"

"Now, Sunday..."

"I knew it! Amy will probably bring that disgusting, old owl with her!"

I shoved myself away from the table and ran into the den, hot tears pricking my eyes.

Dad followed me and stood over me as I huddled in the corner of the sofa.

"Come on, Sunday."

The tears ran down my cheeks. "I don't want

them at my graduation! I don't want them living here!"

I buried my face in the sofa cushion.

"They won't be living here," Dad said quietly.

I looked up, full of dread. "We have to go live at *Marcie's?*" My voice went high. "That means I won't be going to Tarzana High next fall!"

I wanted to die. Julie and I had planned on going to Tarzana High forever.

Dad knelt down and put his arm around me.

"Honey, it won't be that bad. You'll only stay at Marcie's while we're away. And Winnie will be there with you and Amy. When we get back, we'll look for another place downtown. Marcie has to be near the Fashion Mart for work. You know I've wanted to put this place up for sale, anyway."

I clutched Dad and cried into his knitted sweater. "No, no. Please no," I begged. "Tell me I won't have to leave Tarzana."

Finally, Dad murmured, "Sunday, you know I love you. But some things change. You must have felt this coming the last few months. I've been trying to break it to you for weeks. The changes won't be bad in the end. I'm counting on you."

"Don't," I interrupted. "Just don't count

on me for anything. Okay?"

"But I have to." Dad was firm. "While we're away, you must—"

"Count me out of baby-sitting Amy."

"Sunday, don't use that tone."

It was hopeless. "Marry who you want." I jumped up. "Go on a honeymoon. But count me out!" I ran to the back door and ran out of the house.

I heard Dad call after me, "Sunday, come back here! You can't keep running away!"

*Who couldn't?* I pulled my bike out of the garage and took off down the driveway.

"You're a traitor. You said you'd never marry. You're a traitor!" I yelled.

"Sunday! Sunday!" Dad shouted after me.

"Lies. It was all lies!"

Just as I turned the corner, I looked back to see Dad watching me. He was slumped in the doorway, looking confused. "Oh, Daddy," I sobbed.

I rode around for an hour. But the familiar streets made me feel worse. Soon, instead of the woodsy smell of Tarzana, I'd be smelling nothing but car fumes—downtown Los Angeles car fumes.

I finally ended up at Julie's. She would help. Maybe she would have some ideas on having Marcie and Amy kidnapped.

My bike swerved into her driveway, almost knocking down Julie's brother Carl, who was bouncing a ball on the cement.

"Hey, Sunday!" he yelled, as I propped my bike against the garage door. "You look like you're about ready to kill someone."

I ignored him and went into the house to find Julie.

She was in the living room, munching on an apple and reading. She looked up from her book and said, "Hi!"

"Hi," I said, sighing.

"Uh-oh. So, what happened last night?"

"Julie," I paused dramatically. "You were right."

Julie threw down her book. "You've got to be kidding."

"I wish I were kidding. But that's not all. They're going on some dumb honeymoon cruise and leaving me behind with that brat."

Julie gasped, "Oh, no!"

"Oh, yes. I have to stay with her and their stupid English housekeeper for four whole weeks. I have to stay in Marcie's condo!"

Julie's jaw dropped. "But that's downtown! We'll never get to see each other."

"We're going to move downtown." I slumped down on a chair and sobbed. "Julie, what am I going to do?"

Over the next couple of weeks I tried to explain to my dad how I felt. He was as understanding as ever. But when I tried to change his mind about Marcie, I hit a brick wall. I couldn't even get him to reconsider Marcie and Amy coming to my graduation.

When graduation night arrived, I felt defeated.

"Dad, this is my night," I told him as I zipped up the skirt to my blue orchestra uniform. "I don't want to share it with anyone else."

"Of course, it's your night, Sunday," he said, coming over and helping me knot my tie. "We *all* want to hear you play your solo."

I brushed my long hair so hard that static crackled. "Daddy, can't it be just you?"

He shook his head.

"I don't see why not."

"Marcie and Amy really care about you, Sunday. They want to hear you play."

The horn of Julie's dad's car broke the uncomfortable silence. "I guess I'd better go." I picked up my flute. "Bye, Dad."

Dad pulled me to him and kissed my cheek. "Bye, sweetheart. You sure look pretty tonight."

I smiled at him and ran downstairs and out of the house.

Later, waiting for my cue to play my flute, I thought of Dad out in the audience. It gave me courage. But my legs still shook as I walked across the stage.

The auditorium was full, and the cameras were popping. I couldn't see anyone out there in the darkness. I was so nervous!

Trembling, I squinted and peered again. Dad's face was the only thing that could get me through this.

Then I saw him. He was right in the front row just like he'd promised! He was wearing his best jacket, and he looked happy and proud, just like I'd imagined.

The only problem was that he had a growth sitting in his lap. It was Amy.

I thought I would die of embarrassment as I watched Amy sitting in Dad's lap, waving Ollie the Owl's knitted wing at me.

There was no way out. The entire student body of Luther Junior High and their parents saw Amy and Ollie make a fool of me.

I tried to catch Dad's eye. I wanted to beg him to make Amy get down from his lap, to get her out of the auditorium. But he wasn't looking at me. As I sat in front of the music stand, he turned his head to hear what Marcie was saying.

Another part of me acted. It opened the

music, put the flute to my lips, and began to play. How that other part played I will never know. I didn't feel the notes. I just played them  mechanically.

My big moment was ruined!

Marcie and Amy had ruined my graduation. The most important event in my school career had been ruined by a stuffed owl!

All I could think of was revenge. But what would I do?

# Three

That night I decided I'd leave home as soon as I was legally old enough. I figured that I had 965 days left to go.

I was even more determined when on Monday night, after playing Mozart to Dad, he started talking about *our future*. He said the marriage would make everyone feel more secure.

"Not me," I told him. "I felt more secure swimming in the school meet with a broken swimsuit strap."

Dad chuckled. "Even when you're a pain, you can make me laugh."

"I won't lose my sense of humor if you let me stay here. Dad, please don't make me take care of Amy."

"Sunday, it's only a month." Dad sighed. "Amy needs you."

I put down my flute and pulled at the

fringes of the sofa cushion. "Yeah, she needs me to take care of Ollie Owl. Why can't that English housekeeper do it?"

"She can. But she'll need your help. And her name is Winnie."

I yanked at the fringes. "She sounds like a horse."

Dad took away the cushion. "You can see for yourself. Marcie is taking you to meet her tomorrow."

My heart sank. "Tomorrow's Saturday! Julie and I are going to the Galleria!" I moaned.

"You'll have to cut it short."

Then I thought of a sure excuse to get me out of it. "But I have to pick out my bridesmaid's dress."

Dad scratched his beard. "That's no problem. Marcie has already done that for you. She put it on hold for you at the bridal store."

It figured that I wouldn't even get to pick out my own dress.

"I'm surprised she didn't get Ollie Owl to pick it out," I muttered under my breath.

"Marcie will meet you outside the mall at noon." Dad patted my knee. "You'll have to change your plans for once."

"I have to call Julie," I muttered, stomping out of the room.

We had only been shopping for an hour

when Julie said, "Let's go eat. I'm starved."
Food was never far from Julie's mind.

I looked at my watch. "Okay. If we don't go
now, we won't get to eat. I have to pick up my
stupid dress before noon."

We took the glass elevator to the fourth
floor eating area, which was called The Pit.

The Pit was a huge circle of tables and
chairs surrounded by 15 fast-food places. You
could find just about anything to eat there.

We went to Potato A-Peel, and I got a
baked potato covered with Monterey Jack
cheese. Julie got some lasagna from Mama's
Spaghetti.

As we were taking our food to the eating
area, a crowd of sixth-grade boys shoved into
me. Chasing each other through the mall was
their idea of fun.

"They're jerks," I muttered. "I'm glad we
graduated from junior high." I pushed away
the feeling of panic I got at the thought of
school next year.

Julie slid onto a plastic bench. "They'd
better not get our school banned from the
mall. Those kids are the pits."

"They're just small pits in a big Pit."

Julie grinned. But suddenly her smile died.
"I'm going to miss your dumb jokes, Sunday."

I looked at the red and blue pattern on her

shirt. "I'm going to miss yours, too."

"Don't worry, Sun. I'll come visit you at Marcie's."

I murmured, "Thanks, Jule."

It felt terrible that our days together were numbered. Why is it that you have no rights when you're 14? It's a terrible age to be.

I mopped up the last of my melted cheese with my potato. "I hate this age. I'm sick of being pushed around!"

"I know it. But there's nothing we can do," Julie said.

"Maybe we can't change our age, but we can sure make things difficult for other people." I brandished my plastic fork in the air. "Why should I let Marcie run my life? I mean, who says that she can make me change schools? And what right does she have to pick out my clothes?"

Julie nodded. "You're right."

I crushed my empty paper cup with my fist. "I just have to figure out a way to show her."

"How about wearing jeans to the wedding, like you suggested the other day?"

I shook my head. "I can't hurt Dad that way. No, I have to think of something better than that." I piled my things onto the cardboard tray. "I'll play along with Marcie. She won't suspect a thing."

"But what will you do?"

"I don't know. But it's got to be something as mean as ruining a person's graduation. Come on. You can help me think of something while we're picking up the stupid dress."

But the moment we saw the dress, our spirits were crushed. It was baby pink, and looped with bows and flowers from the puffed sleeves to the frilled hem.

"Oh, no." I groaned.

Mute with misery, we studied the pink monster hanging on the fitting room door.

Then Julie fingered the fitted bodice and puffed sleeves. "I thought Marcie had better taste."

"She picked this to annoy me."

"Try it on," Julie urged. "Maybe it won't be so bad once it's on."

Choking back angry tears, I pulled off my jeans and shirt and dragged the dress over my head.

It was unbelievable. The dress looked worse on me than on the hanger. Staring at my reflection, I began to feel sick. I had never looked so long and thin. My arms hung from the sleeves like two sticks.

But worse than that was the tight, flattening bodice.

Didn't Marcie know that tight bodices and

full skirts were the worst thing for people who were trying to keep their chest size a secret?

Julie shook her dark curls sympathetically. "Take it off."

I turned sideways. My chest looked as flat as Amy's. I was so mad that I thought I might scream.

As Julie jerked on the zipper, my anger burst from me. "I *won't* wear this dress!" I stepped out and kicked at the skirt drifting to the floor. "I am going to choose my own dress."

"Yay for Sunday!" encouraged Julie. She slid the dress back onto its padded hanger.

Hastily, I pulled on my own clothes. "Julie, give it to me. I'm going to show Marcie who's boss."

I marched out of the fitting room, trailing the long pink dress from its hanger.

"I'm sorry," I told the surprised, gray-haired saleswoman as I handed her the dress. "This dress isn't right. Could we see some others?"

"Well, I..." She smoothed down the folds of the skirt nervously.

"It's okay. My mother told me to pick out what I wanted."

"This was on hold for..." She looked at the tag that was pinned to the skirt, "Mrs. Vane. It's a bridesmaid's..."

"No, no," I interrupted hastily. "It's my prom dress." I fixed her puzzled frown with a wide-eyed look. Maybe she thought I was too young to be graduating. "My junior prom," I added, airily.

"Oh..."

"I need something less fancy, a little more..."

"Prom-like?" she suggested, tilting her gray head to one side.

"Right." I flashed her a smile.

"Well, our prom gowns are in the other case."

"I'd like to see them." I walked purposefully over to the glass case.

"Well, if you're sure," she murmured reluctantly. "These are our latest styles." She slid open the glass doors to a row of prom dresses.

"I'll try this," I touched a pale blue one, "and this..."

Julie and I picked out five of the most gorgeous dresses. "I've never had so much fun in my life," I whispered as we skipped into the dressing room for the second time.

"Neither have I," Julie said. "I can't wait to see you in the lilac one."

I felt like a princess as I slipped first into the lilac dress, and then into the blue one, and next into the pale yellow dress.

But when I put on the fourth dress, I felt like a queen. It was perfect.

"You look so grown up," said Julie, admiringly.

"Do you really think so?" I twirled in front of the long mirror, making the soft silk float. "Julie, I really want it."

"It's beautiful," Julie breathed. "But, Sunday, what would Marcie say?" asked Julie.

I shrugged my shoulders. "She's not my mother."

"I know, but—do you think you should wear *that* color?"

"Why not?" I felt brave and strong. "It's a whole lot better than a color I stopped wearing when I was three."

"I know, but—"

"Julie, Marcie ruined my graduation. Why should I do what she wants me to for her wedding?"

"I guess you're right," said Julie doubtfully.

"I am right." I looked at my watch. "Come on. She's picking me up in twenty minutes. Undo me."

Shaking her head, Julie helped me out of the dress.

As I carried my dream dress to the saleswoman, I felt determined and powerful.

But my strength did not last. An hour later,

slumped in the white leather seat of Marcie's Porsche, I wasn't sure I had done the right thing.

The dress was stuffed under my seat in a garment bag.

Marcie frowned. "Sunday, you'll crease the dress if you put it down there. Lay it on the backseat."

I obeyed with a pounding heart. What if she asked to see inside the package?

"How do you like it?" Marcie asked.

"I like it fine," I said shortly.

"Amy looks as cute as a button in it. You two will make wonderful twin bridesmaids."

*Twins!* Of course, that was why Marcie picked such a little girl dress. It suited Amy.

Right then I was glad that I switched dresses. Marcie deserved it. I bent my head down and traced the stitching of my jeans with my finger, pleased that my jeans looked dirty against the perfect car interior.

After a long silence, Marcie cleared her throat and said, "Sunday, I'd like us to get to know each other."

I didn't answer.

"Can we talk?"

"What do you want to talk about?"

"I want to talk to you about Winnie."

"What about her?"

She swallowed. "She...she has bad migraine headaches. I hope you'll be quiet around her. Try not to be put off by her funny ways." She carefully steered her car through the downtown traffic.

"What funny ways?" I unwrapped a candy bar that I'd bought at the mall.

"Do you have to eat candy in my car?" Marcie looked worriedly at the white seats.

I ignored her and took a bite of the candy bar. "What funny ways?"

Marcie's manicured fingers tightened on the wheel. "Sunday, let's try to get along."

I didn't answer. I'd never get along with her.

Marcie shook her head. "Okay. Have it your way. But I want you to understand that Winnie is...well...different."

Roughly translated that could mean she had two heads.

"How different?"

Marcie drove into her condo parking lot.

"I guess it's because she's English," she turned her lipstick-smeared smile on me. "But I'm sure you'll get on the right side of her."

"Sure, no problem," I muttered. "Just call me Supergirl."

I opened the car door with my left hand, the sticky one.

# *Four*

The lobby of Marcie's building was unreal. It was painted in pastels, and it had a huge mirror covering one wall. There was a fake chandelier hanging from the cottage cheese ceiling. Ceilings like that were something Dad and I once laughed at together.

We rode the elevator in silence.

As Marcie opened the door to her condo, I wanted to run.

Was this really the place where I was going to live? It was like an ad for capped teeth—white, perfect, and phony. The furniture was white leather with a glass-topped table standing on chrome legs. There were two black lamps that reminded me of spiders. An empty white canvas hung on the wall.

It suited Marcie perfectly.

I followed her to the kitchen with its smooth white cupboards and bare, black-tile counters. I wished it was a picture in a magazine.

Then I could rip it out and burn it.

My thoughts were interrupted by Marcie speaking in a cheerful voice that, to me, sounded really fake.

"Sunday, this is Winnie."

I stared at the person in front of me. An enormous body in a wrap-around, flowered apron was kneeling on the floor, scrubbing. I couldn't see its head or front—just this huge bottom, moving in time with the arm.

"Mind my clean floor," ordered a voice, behind the bottom.

"Winnie, this is Sunday," Marcie said in a firm voice.

"It's Saturday. I always do my floors on Saturday."

*Great. Now I was just a day of the week,* I thought.

Marcie laughed. "No, this is Sunday Moon. She's here to meet you."

The flowered mountain heaved up off the floor.

I have a habit of giggling when I'm nervous, and the sight of that flowered bottom started me off. The hat didn't help.

I really think that even a non-nervous person would laugh if they saw someone wearing a fake-fur hat in a kitchen in the middle of summer.

"What's so funny?" boomed Winnie. "Don't you teenagers learn any manners?"

I gulped my laughter down.

"And look at what you've done!" She pointed a finger at the floor. "You've messed up my clean floor!"

I looked down at my sneakers. They were filthy.

I wanted to go home. I wanted to pack and run away.

Turning on my dirty heel, I ran out of the perfect kitchen and out of the perfect apartment.

All the way home in the car, I planned to tell Dad that I wasn't ever going back to Marcie's. I would tell him that I was going to live at Julie's house.

But when I got home, I didn't get the chance. He was sitting on the sofa with Amy curled up beside him. And one of his arms was around her.

I swallowed hard when I saw what was happening. My dad was teaching Amy how to play his flute!

"Okay, sweetheart," Dad was saying. "First you press here to sound the note."

As a little girl, having Dad teach me to play the flute was my special thing. How could he do the same for *her?*

"Hi, you two," Marcie said sweetly, coming in behind me.

Dad looked up. "Hi!" He smiled and got up. "So, how'd it go?"

He put his arm around my shoulders, but his eyes were fastened on Marcie's face.

"We did just fine, Joe," lied Marcie. "How about you two? Did you get to know each other a little more?"

Dad smiled. "We sure did. Didn't we, Amy?"

"Uh-huh," Amy said happily.

"She's a great kid, Marcie," Dad said.

I moved away from Dad and swallowed.

"I'm glad you think so. You're pretty wonderful yourself."

Then, right in front of me, just like that, they hugged each other!

"Sunday, honey. Come here." Dad held out one arm. "I want you to know how happy I am that we'll be a real family at last."

I wanted to shout that we already were a real family! But instead I just stared.

"Sunday, I'm so glad we'll be together," Marcie said softly. "I've always wanted a big sister for Amy."

*Yuck.*

"You can teach me how to cook all of your dad's favorite dishes. It's time you had some fun—"

"I have plenty of fun already."

Marcie still had that gooey look on her face. "Well, I mean, you won't have to worry about housework with Winnie and—"

"We don't need a maid."

Dad moved over to me and encircled me in his arms. "Come on, Sunday Mouse. Marcie is just trying to tell you that she wants to be friends."

*Friends!* I wanted to scream. But instead I buried my face in Dad's sweater. For his sake, I guess, I had to try.

"I'm glad you're happy, Dad," I murmured brokenly.

"That's my girl," he whispered, stroking my head.

For a second I wished I hadn't chosen the other dress.

But only for a second. Marcie deserved it, didn't she?

Anyway, unless I did a miracle dye job or went stark naked, I was stuck with it.

The stupid wedding was next week.

# *Five*

I couldn't believe it. The awful, dreadful wedding was actually here.

It was being held in our backyard. Marcie had managed to get rid of anything wild or natural back there. The battered patio furniture had been replaced with rows of white, rental chairs. There were displays of flowers arranged by a florist, but all the ones that grew wild in our yard had been chopped down.

I stared out the kitchen window at my tree house. Dad and I had made that tree house four summers ago. It's a great place to hide out. I've even slept in it during the summer a few times.

But today it looked ridiculous. Balloons hung from the branches. And the tree house was tied with a big, yellow ribbon.

Dad was in the den, fiddling with the stereo system. He was planning to have Beatles music piped over the whole yard.

"Sunday, aren't you dressed yet?" he called.

I sauntered into the den.

"I thought I'd go this way." I stuck my thumb in my jeans pockets.

Dad smiled. "You are supposed to wear a dress, remember?"

I sighed. "I remember, Dad."

We had made a deal that if I wore a dress, he would wear a suit. I really thought it would be great if he wore old clothes. Thinking of that promise made me feel nervous. I went slowly to my room to get ready.

My heart thudded as I locked the door behind me and took out my dress. Nobody but Julie had seen it. And she was sworn to secrecy. I felt as nervous as if I were the bride. *Should I go through with my plan?* I wondered.

I pulled off my clothes and went into the bathroom. Maybe I could stay in the shower during the whole ceremony.

I dried myself off and took the dress off the hanger. Smoothing down the shining folds of the skirt, I sighed. It was a beautiful dress. But was it right for me to wear it?

Well, it was too late now. Determinedly, I pulled it over my head.

A half hour later, I walked slowly and

shakily downstairs to where Marcie, Amy, and Marcie's dad waited.

I trembled on the last step and thought about running back upstairs. But then Marcie turned around. She was wearing a long, white wedding gown, complete with a veil. A glowing smile was fixed on her face. But when she saw my dress, the smile froze. She stared at me in horror.

"I don't believe it!" she whispered.

I hid my shaking hands in the lace overskirt of my dress. "You don't believe what?"

Marcie's words burned through me like acid. "Where is your bridesmaid's dress?" Her voice got louder. "The pink dress that I picked out!"

"It didn't fit me. It—"

"Sunday Moon, what do you think you're doing?" she whispered.

"Nothing—I—"

Amy danced around me in her pink dress. "Sunday's a bride, Sunday's a bride," she sang out.

"Be quiet," I whispered furiously. "I am not."

Marcie brought her face close to mine. "Don't you know that only the bride wears white?" She touched the glistening white sleeve of my dress. "I can't believe it! You

46

are actually wearing a bridal gown!"

I stepped back, scared. Her fury was awful. "It is not. It's a prom dress. L-leave me alone."

For a long, terrible moment we just stared at one another.

Outside the trumpet fanfare started for the beginning of the ceremony.

Marcie said in a determined voice, "I can't deal with you now, Sunday. I want to be your friend, but you're making it very difficult." She shook her dark head. "This is my wedding day." Turning to her father she said, "Daddy, are you ready to give me away?" She pulled down her veil and stepped out into the sunlight.

At that moment I wished I had worn a veil. Then I could have hidden behind it. Rigidly, I stepped into our backyard to the sound of the wedding march. Somehow the ceremony began.

I thought all they had to say was "I do," but Dad and Marcie made whole speeches.

Marcie talked in a soft voice about how lucky she was to have met someone as warm and caring as my dad.

Dad talked about his life being complete. He said he hoped to make a fine husband to Marcie and a loving father to his girls.

Silently, I cried. The tears ran down my

cheeks. *Daddy, you're mine. Why do I have to share you?* I cried to myself.

Maybe the guests thought I was just being sentimental. What did they know? Had they ever seen their future crumbling before them in just a few minutes? My life with Dad, my home, my friends, my school were all being dragged from me with every second.

Finally, it was time for the pictures.

"Sunday," Dad pleaded, "at least smile for the pictures, will you?"

I choked down a sob and tried to smile.

"Look at me, Daddy," demanded Amy. "I'm smiling."

Marcie took me to one side.

"Don't rock the boat anymore, Sunday," she whispered as the guests gathered under the flowered arches for the photographs. "Let's call a truce. For your dad's sake. Please?"

I forced the muscles in my face to smile. Victory did not taste sweet.

Marcie had spoiled my graduation. She deserved to have her wedding day ruined. But I didn't feel good doing it.

The person I was about to live with, Winnie, was on the end of the row posing for pictures. She was wearing a red, spotted outfit and a hat that looked like a wedding cake. I'm surprised she didn't have the happy bride and groom stuck on top.

When the pictures were done, she waddled over to me.

"What have we here?" She fingered my dress disapprovingly.

I jerked away. "Don't—"

"I told Mrs. Fairchild that teenagers were nothing but trouble." The spots on her dress jiggled as she shook her head.

*You don't know the meaning of trouble,* I thought to myself. *Just wait till my dad's not around.*

We were interrupted by Julie's voice calling, "Sunday! Hi!"

I looked away from Winnie to see Julie waving at me.

"Come get something to eat before there's nothing left!" shouted Julie.

As I hurried over to Julie, Winnie called after me, "You shouldn't be wearing a white dress, by rights! Only the bride wears white."

"And you shouldn't be wearing red spots," I muttered. "Only a circus clown wears red spots."

"Who is that?" Julie whispered, moving toward the buffet table.

"*That* is Winnie."

"Her hat—" Julie started to giggle.

I stuffed some cheese sticks into my mouth.

"I know. I think it affects her brain."

"It looks like the hat exploded," Julie giggled as she loaded her plate with food.

I looked over at the lace tiers bursting from the hat on Winnie's head.

"Yeah," I muttered. "A volcanic brain eruption."

Julie broke up.

I had to laugh, too. When I saw Winnie's mountainous behind bending over Amy, I laughed even more. "Look at L.A.'s answer to Mount St. Helen," I snorted, sending out a spray of cheese crumbs.

Julie shrieked with laughter.

I nearly choked on the cheese sticks. But it felt good.

What would happen when Julie wasn't around to laugh with? Tomorrow my dad was leaving. I would be left alone with Winnie and Amy.

I looked over at them. Which one should I murder first?

# Six

I didn't think anything could be worse than Dad's wedding day. But the next day he was leaving, and I was moving in to Marcie's condo.

It was worse than the wedding.

My insides churned like crazy, and I kept having to go to the bathroom.

When it was time to leave, I couldn't bear to say good-bye to my room. It hurt too much. I just closed my door on all my collections, my posters, and my furniture. My life was over.

I didn't even get to ride over alone with Dad. My legs were too long to fit around all the luggage that we had piled into the station wagon. So, Amy got to go with my Dad, and I got to go with Marcie.

I think Amy was the only one happy with the arrangement. She thought Dad was her own father these days.

In the car, Marcie informed me that for now I'd be sharing a room with Amy. Amy was too nervous to sleep alone while Marcie was away, and besides, Marcie didn't have time to clear out her darkroom before the wedding.

I didn't say a word. Even a black-walled room that smelled of chemicals was better than sharing a room with Amy. But who cared what I thought?

Marcie went on about my moving in as if this was the most exciting day of my life. "Sharing a room with Amy will help you get to know her. I know you'll learn to love her, Sunday. She just adores you already."

I just stared out the car window, mournfully noting the built-up skyline looming ahead. Marcie babbled on, but I phased her out of my thoughts.

As soon as we pulled into the parking lot, I jumped out of the car, dragging my backpack and flute with me.

I waited upstairs for Dad, and when he came into the apartment, I dragged him into Amy's room.

"Daddy, let me come with you," I begged. "I'll be a stowaway."

"I'm sorry, Sunday. You have to stay here." He hugged me. "I'm going to miss you a lot, sweetheart, but I know you'll be all right."

I clung to him. "Don't go. Don't go. Stay with me."

Dad stroked my hair. "I can't, Sunday, but you know I love you."

"You love me best, right Daddy?" I asked tearfully.

"Honey, love doesn't stop. It grows with the more people you love," he whispered.

That wasn't the answer I wanted to hear.

As soon as we'd unloaded my stuff, the taxi arrived to take Dad and Marcie to the docks.

Marcie kissed Amy. Amy screamed. Dad kissed me and promised to write, and then he kissed Amy. And then, before I knew it, they were gone.

I wished I could scream and kick like Amy. But I wasn't four. I was 14.

I ran to Amy's room, quietly sobbing. *Daddy, Daddy come back. Don't leave me here,* I cried to myself over and over. But he didn't hear. And would he come back even if he did hear?

I don't know how long I cried, but it seemed like forever.

When I felt sick from it, I lifted my head and looked around the room.

I never had to share a room before. I was going to hate it. All the toys were stacked around the room on shelves. Every toy seemed to have a pair of eyes watching me. Even the walls were bordered with rows of owls wearing glasses—Ollie's relatives, I guessed.

My bed was a trundle bed that was pulled out from underneath Amy's. It was high and narrow with an orange blanket stretched tightly across it. It reminded me of those bunk beds at camp. And it felt like an ironing board.

Just then, I heard Winnie plodding down the hall.

"Are you in there, Miss Bride?"

She thought it was funny to call me that ever since the wedding.

I didn't answer.

"I said, are you in there? Dinner's ready!" she bellowed.

"I'm not hungry!" I yelled back.

She sniffled. "Suit yourself." I heard her muttering, "Teenagers," to herself as she waddled back to the kitchen.

There used to be a show on TV about an English nanny and a professor. The nanny was cute and blond. She solved everyone's problems. I always wanted her to come live with me. And what did I get instead? Winnie.

I pulled my notebook and the list of honeymoon ports from my bag. I hunched my knees up and rested the notepad against them. I decided to write my first letter to my dad. *There's nothing else to do around here,* I thought.

*Dear Daddy,*
*I miss you. It's only been an hour since you left, but already I miss you. Is that dumb? Do you miss me? We've never been separated before, except for Camp Arrowhead.*

Someone tapped on the door.
"Who is it?" I yelled
"Sunday Moon, I want to show you Ollie Owl. He—"
"Go away, Amy."
"Ollie wants to show you—"
"I'm busy. Go play."
She started to whimper. She got cranky whenever she didn't get her way.
Winnie called to Amy from the kitchen. "What's the matter? Won't that mean sister play with you? Come to Winnie, and get a cookie."
*I hope it chokes you.*
I hated them both. And I wasn't anybody's sister.
I carried on with my letter:

*I wish you weren't so far away. Dad, I hate to tell you this, but Winnie bribes Amy with cookies. I don't think that's right, do you? And you wouldn't believe how Amy turns on the phony crying. She stops the second she gets a cookie.*

*Helping out with her won't be easy. I'm glad you never bribed me, because I grew up realizing that I couldn't have everything I wanted. I don't want to make you feel bad, but I didn't want you to get married or leave me here. I want to go back home to Tarzana. And, Daddy, I don't want to go to L.A. High. They have gangs there. Isn't that scary?*

*I will try to make the best of it while you're away. I guess I have no choice (ha, ha). I will practice my flute every day. And I'll write to you, like I promised. Please write back. Please come home soon, Daddy. But enjoy your vacation, anyway.*

*I love you, Daddy,*

*Your One and Only Daughter,*
*Sunday Moon*

I figured I'd better put that bit about "One and Only Daughter" because he seemed to be forgetting that lately.

I wondered how long it would take for the letter to reach him. After sealing it in an envelope, I addressed it and stuck on a stamp.

Sneaking past the kitchen, I saw Winnie and Amy eating dinner in there. It smelled terrible.

The elevator took me down to the lobby. There was a mailbox right outside the building.

I gave Dad's letter a little kiss, and I pushed it into the mailbox. It made me feel better to know that Dad would be holding that same envelope soon. If I could stick a big stamp on my behind and post myself with it, I'd feel even better.

Slowly, I walked back to the elevator. A whole month to live through before I saw Dad again. But I'd see plenty of El Bratto and Mary Poppins.

Then I saw something that made me forget my misery, at least for a while. Leaning against the lobby wall, by the elevator, was a boy. He was about 16, and he was tall, with long legs and light brown hair. He was carrying a music case that was covered with stickers. Tapping the case, he hummed to himself.

He was so lost in his music that he didn't notice me. Naturally, I didn't have the guts to get close enough so that I could read the stickers.

What a dud I am when it comes to boys. Instead of taking the elevator, I took the stairs. But I almost ran up the stairs as I thought about the boy I'd just seen. He was a musician, and he was right in this building. Maybe he lives here!

The apartment was quiet when I slipped back inside. I ran to my room and closed the door. Jumping onto the bed, I scrunched up in the corner and clutched the blanket to my chin.

There's a trick I learned while waiting at the dentist. You try to concentrate on nice things and block out the nasty stuff. I thought of my collections back home. Collecting things is my hobby. Dad says I am a regular pack rat. Anything pretty goes into my collection. Stones, stickers, rubber stamps, pretty boxes, and anything miniature. My miniature craze started when Dad built me a dollhouse. I don't tell people because they might think I am immature, but I still love my dollhouse.

Then I thought of the Bendy family.

The Bendy family lives in my dollhouse. Mr. Bendy sits in the armchair reading the newspaper, Mrs. Bendy carries ceramic platters of food, and Wendy Bendy practices ballet. The Bendys are a very traditional family.

When I was little, I used to dream of being Wendy Bendy. She had a mother, a father, and a brother. She was pretty, too, with her rubber hair painted yellow and a blue dress. She was always smiling, no matter what, even when I bent her into difficult ballet poses. But she didn't like it when I tipped the house over to dump out the furniture.

Now I felt like Wendy Bendy. It was like some giant hand had shaken my house and had dumped me in some alien place. I felt horrible.

Thinking about my collections was not helping me forget everything else. There was only one thing left to try. I leaned over the bed and picked up my flute. Playing my flute always makes me feel better. Just as I got into playing my scales, the door flew open. I jumped about six miles.

Winnie stood there, panting. She looked like a real dreamboat in her curlers, hairnet, and bathrobe.

"That noise is giving me a migraine headache, and Amy needs to get to bed," she complained. "Put that thing away."

Noise! How dare she! Anyway, I thought her slamming the door and thudding down the hall was more likely to disturb people than my playing.

Amy came into the room and climbed into bed then. "I want my Mommy," she whimpered.

*Well, I don't,* I thought.

Winnie came back in. This place was like a train station.

"Now you just go to sleep, dear. Mommy will be back soon," Winnie cooed as she tucked Amy in.

Then she turned to me and said in a gruff voice, "Lights out now."

She wasn't put off by my slit, gray-eyed look. She simply flipped off the light switch, leaving me with nothing but a night-light!

How dare she be so rude? I almost screamed. I wasn't even undressed.

This was not going to work.

Undressing in the dark, I thought of all the people I hated—Marcie, Amy, Carl Essentia, and now Winnie. The list was growing.

Somehow I didn't think it was the growth that Dad was always talking about.

# Seven

I was dreaming about ways to get rid of Marcie when a noise woke me up.

"Ollie wants to go to the park," announced Amy in a piercing voice, swinging on the door. She was wearing Snoopy pajamas with feet.

I squinted in the morning sun.

"Owls don't like the daylight," I growled.

"Ollie does."

I turned my back to her. "Go away."

"Please, please, please—" Something tickled my ear. "Ollie wants to kiss you."

I felt his beak peck at my ear lobe. Amy sure knew how to get her own way. *Who could reason with an owl?* I thought.

Anyway, it was a chance to get some exercise. I needed to be in good shape when I ran away from this place. Groaning, I rolled out of bed. Amy watched me as I pulled on my clothes. Then she asked me to help her get dressed.

"I thought kids your age dressed themselves," I told her, as I tied her shoelaces.

"Huh-uh. My mommy helps me."

We crept out of the apartment. The sight of Winnie in her bathrobe was more than I could take just then.

Amy grasped my hand as we walked across the street to the park. I really couldn't pull it away. It was necessary for safety.

The park was not like the parks in Tarzana. The ones there had huge tracks and baseball diamonds. But this one was more like a natural parkland. It had lots of trees, and even a duck pond with real ducks swimming in it. In the city, you need some kind of nature I figured.

It was so early that it was still chilly. No one else was crazy enough to be there, except for a few joggers. I did a couple of warm-up exercises. That way nobody would think I was nuts.

Amy played on the slide. She kept waving to me as she slid down.

It reminded me of when I was a little girl. I loved going to playgrounds with Dad. We'd spend all morning there sometimes. Dad would read the newspaper, and I would play on the swings and the slide.

It was sad to think that I'd never have him to myself like that again. I wanted to go back to being that little girl again.

I wondered why I had to grow up.

I looked up at the slide. Putting my foot on the bottom step, I paused. Maybe I was too big. But since there was no one around, I climbed up. I wedged myself onto the slippery slope and took off.

"Dandy! Out of the way, dummy!" I heard somebody yell to the dog heading my way.

But it was too late. The dumb dog jumped and barked at the bottom of the slide waiting for me to come down and play. I landed on his back, fanny first.

"Ouch!"

There was enough yowling to wake the whole downtown, but I'm not sure who was yelping most—me or the dog.

"Dandy, stay! Are you okay? Dandy, stay!"

But Dandy wasn't sticking around to be sat on. He beat it.

"You came down so fast that I couldn't stop him," Dandy's owner told me, in an amused voice.

It was the elevator boy! If only the sandbox would have opened up and swallowed me.

His blue eyes twinkled. "I guess Dandy

thought you were playing."

I looked at his face and tried to smile in a glamorous, adult way. That was all I needed—a sore behind and Mr. Music Man thinking I was a kid.

"Well, if you're okay—my name's Eric. Eric Calvert!" he called as he ran after the golden retriever. "Come back, Dandy, you big oaf!"

Eric Calvert. *Swoon!* He was the best-looking boy I'd ever *not* talked to.

"Poor Sunday," said Amy. "Ollie will kiss it and make it better."

Some girls get boys kissing them. I get owls.

"It's okay. No, thanks."

"Does it hurt?"

"I'm okay." Why did Eric Calvert have to see me act like a little kid? I bet he thought I was an idiot child.

"Come on, Amy. Let's go back."

Winnie was waiting in the doorway for us when we got back.

"I was just about to call the police!" she gasped. "I was so worried. Where on earth have you been?"

"We went to the park, and Sunday hurt her—" Amy started.

Winnie grabbed me by my shoulders before I could get past.

"Wait a minute, miss."

I pulled away. "Let go."

But Winnie wouldn't let go. "Don't you ever do that again! You almost gave me a heart attack. If you were mine, I'd put you across my knee."

My heart beat fast. "You wouldn't dare!"

She wagged her fat finger in my face. "It's high time that you got some discipline. Your father has spoiled you rotten."

I swallowed. She had no right to talk to me like that. "Let me by, please," I demanded in a cool voice.

That took the air out of the old windbag.

"Just don't ever do that again," she repeated in a quieter voice. "I was worried sick. My nerves—"

She turned and followed Amy down the hall.

That was all the thanks I got for getting up at dawn, injuring myself, and ruining my chances with a boy!

Forget baby-sitting. Forget living here. I was leaving!

I told that to Dad in a letter. I said that I would give him a forwarding address when I had one. I hoped it was something better than "Second Park Bench Next To The Trash Cans." I told him about Winnie threatening to hit me, too.

When I was finished, I was so hungry that

I went into the kitchen. I'd been up since six, and I hadn't eaten a scrap of food. They were starving me here on top of everything else!

Winnie was cooking something in a skillet. I won't say what it looked like, but I think it was sausages. I can't stand meat in the morning.

"Sit down, and have some breakfast," she ordered.

"I'll make my own." I took a box of cereal and filled a bowl.

"Miss Independence," she grumbled to herself.

Amy was sitting next to Ollie Owl, who was wearing a bib. The way he dropped his food, he needed it. "Ollie wants to say hi. Say hi to Ollie," she instructed.

I just ignored her.

I hated this place. I wanted my own things, my own friends. Most of all, I wanted Julie.

After breakfast, I dialed her number.

The phone rang eight times before it was picked up.

"Hello?" I called into the receiver.

"Sunday, how are you?"

It was Mrs. Essentia. Next to Dad, she was my second favorite adult in the world.

"I'm awful. I miss Julie, and—"

"Well, come over, dear. Julie's so busy

66

yelling at her brother that it might be the only way you'll get to talk to her."

"Uh-oh." I said with a giggle. It felt strange to laugh.

"It's called sibling love." Mrs. Essentia sighed. "You must tell me all about your sibling rivalry later, dear. Here's Julie."

She handed the phone to Julie before I had a chance to remind her that I wasn't a sibling.

"Hi." Julie was breathless.

"Hi."

Julie announced for the hundredth time, "I hate that Carl." It was a relief to know that some things never change.

"I thought you were crazy about him," I joked.

"Huh?" Julie giggled. "So, how's it going with Superbrat?"

She meant Amy, of course. "It's terrible. I'm running away."

Julie groaned. "Why don't you come over? Ask my mom if you can live with us. Carl won't be here, thank goodness. He's going over to Dan's today."

A wave of relief came over me as I thought about Julie's house, safe and secure. "I'll get showered and be right over," I told Julie. "How long does it take on the bus?"

"About an hour, I think. I'll ask my mom if it's okay. MOM!"

I jumped. Julie has a habit of shouting to other people while she still has me on the line. She almost breaks my eardrum sometimes.

She yelled again at her mom. "Okay, okay–"

"She wants me to apologize to Carl first. The things I do just to see you."

"I'm worth it," I told her. "I'll see you later." I hung up and went to get my things.

When I was ready, I took a note into the kitchen. Winnie was at the kitchen table reading one of those newspapers that you buy at supermarket checkouts.

"Single parent families on the increase," she read. "Single parent families are to blame for today's youth, if you ask me."

I hadn't asked her. I didn't care what her opinion of anything was.

"Here's Julie's phone number." I handed her a slip of paper. "I'm going there. You can call her mother to check if you want."

Winnie sniffled. "Miss Independence, you'd better take a key," she said, getting me one from the drawer. "I don't want you waking me up at all hours."

She didn't have to worry. I wasn't even coming back.

Amy ran up to me as I was leaving. "I want

68

to come! I want to come," she whined.

"No," I said. "Go play with Ollie."

I ran down the stairs before she could say anything else.

# Eight

The bus ride to Julie's took forever. It went through streets I never even knew existed. Los Angeles is so big that you can grow up in one area without ever passing through others.

In one part there were rows of broken-down buildings covered with graffiti. Kids played around old sofas and garbage cans. There were a lot of kids.

One girl who looked about six years old was carrying a little boy. She puffed and stopped every few seconds to hoist him up. The little girl wasn't much older than Amy. Just watching her made me feel bad. If that little kid could be so responsible, I should be too. But Amy was impossible. If she wasn't such a whiner, I would take care of her. But there was no way I could be nice to such a pain.

Still, I felt guilty. I'd promised Dad that

I'd watch Amy, and already I was letting him down. Fairchilds kept their promises, even tough ones. I looked out the bus window. The little girl was gone now, but Amy was still on my mind. I pulled myself up in the bus seat. I always kept my promises. This time was not going to be any different. Even if Amy was the pain of the century, she was my responsibility.

I couldn't let Dad down, although trying to take care of Amy was going to be hard. Amy was such a pest. I took out my pad and pen from my bag and began to write a letter to Dad. It was hard to write while the bus was moving, but Dad would like what I had to say.

I told him about taking Amy to the park. I told him what Winnie had said and that she had called me names. Then, to prove how adult I was, I mentioned that I would still watch Amy. As I wrote that I wondered if he was thinking of me. Probably not. I figured that at that moment he was probably entering a knobby knees contest or whatever it is they do on cruise ships.

The bus reached the end of Julie's street just as I signed the letter, "Your Number One Daughter." I gathered together my things and jumped off the bus to greet the familiar smell of Tarzana.

It was wonderful. It felt good to mail that letter and walk up the road to Julie's house.

Julie was sitting on her front lawn making a sketch of her house when I walked up.

She squinted her brown eyes in the sunlight as she looked up. "Hi."

"Hi." I flopped down beside her and looked at her sketch. "That's good."

She held the drawing at arm's length. "Do you think so? We have to do three pieces for homework this week. We have to sketch a tree, a person, and a house. So far, the house is the hardest."

I sighed. "I love your house." The words caught in my throat. "I—I love it almost as much as mine."

Julie looked at me. "What's wrong?"

I swallowed. "I wish I could come live here."

Julie put down her sketch pad. "But I thought you were going to live here. I've been working on my mom about it."

I pushed back a long strand of hair and gulped. "Thanks, Julie. But I can't. I have to go back. I promised Dad that I'd help with Amy, and—"

"You and your Fairchild promises." Julie's face was understanding. "Poor Sunday. I was looking forward to you coming."

"I was, too."

Julie leaned forward. "Look, you don't have to be there all the time."

"I guess not. But Winnie is so mean. All she does is complain. If I'm not around to yell at, maybe she'll pick on Amy."

"She yells at you?"

"Yes. She yells at me for everything. I'm not even allowed to practice my flute. If only I could go home." My eyes stung.

Julie put her arm around me. "I know."

"I want my dad and my own room and—" I rubbed my eyes. Julie squeezed my shoulders. "Don't cry, Sunday. You can come visit me as much as you want."

"It's not the same."

"I know." For a moment we were silent. Then Julie said, "Do you want to get some lunch? Everyone gets depressed on an empty stomach."

I nodded. "Okay." I was pretty hungry. "Do you know what else Winnie does?" I asked as I followed Julie into the house.

"What?"

"She cooks doggie doo-doo sausages for breakfast."

"You're kidding!"

"I wish I were kidding. And she expects me to eat them!"

We both broke up.

We were still laughing when we got into the house. Our laughter bounced around the hanging pots in the Essentia kitchen. Mrs. Essentia is a great cook. She's also a great collector, like me. My favorite is her collection of teapots. I love the one that is shaped like a giant ocean liner. But looking at it then made me think of my dad who was so far away. Swallowing the thought, I asked Julie, "What are we going to eat?"

"How about Sunday Moon's famous tuna surprise sandwiches?"

I grinned. "Okay."

While I fixed the sandwiches with the secret ingredient, celery powder, Julie made chocolate shakes and filled a bowl with potato chips.

Lunch was delicious. Julie was right. I felt a lot better after I'd eaten.

"Do you want to try out Carl's new skateboard?" Julie asked, draining the last bit of chocolate shake from her glass.

"Sure." I carried my plate to the sink.

Even though no one was home, we sneaked upstairs to Carl's room. It would be a disaster if he found out.

"Welcome to the city dump!" muttered Julie, flinging open his door.

"It smells terrible in here." There was a stale, locker-room odor coming from the clothes and sports equipment that were thrown everywhere. "My room's messy, but–" I stopped, remembering that I might not ever see my room again. "Come on. Let's find that skateboard and get out of here."

We searched for the skateboard for 10 minutes. Even though it was covered with fluorescent stickers, it was hard to find among the debris. I finally found it under a pile of magazines. Having a brother did have its advantages. You could use his things. But then it meant that he had a right to share yours.

I'd rather be an only child.

We had a great time skateboarding. But we got pretty beaten up on the slopes.

We limped back to Julie's around four.

"Let's get a snack before dinner," said Julie, leading the way to the kitchen.

"No snacks," called Julie's mom. "Dinner's almost ready." She was at the stove cooking.

"Hi, Mom. You're home early." Julie kissed her mom.

Mrs. Essentia has a job doing research at the local museum. She's a real brain. "How are you doing, Sunday?" she asked, hugging me.

"Okay, now that I'm here."

She held her arm around me and gave me

a sympathetic look. "It's really that bad, huh?"

"It's okay." I didn't want to get into it again.

Mrs. Essentia understood. She turned her attention to Julie. "Julie, put that skateboard away before Carl gets here. I can't stand another fight. You'd better cover those battle wounds with pants."

"What, these beautiful legs?" I joked, posing like a star.

"Scabby knees are the latest fashion," Julie said, linking her arm through mine.

Mrs. Essentia laughed. "You two stars can get washed up for dinner."

Dinner that night was delicious. It was my favorite—spaghetti.

In the summer, I eat at the Essentia's a lot. I grow about an inch in every direction from all the food. I love being there. If Carl wasn't around, it would be even better.

Mr. Essentia asked me a lot of questions about the wedding and my dad's cruise. He's a nice man but he sure can talk a lot. Finally, Mrs. Essentia rescued me by asking me to help her get dessert.

"It's your favorite," she told me, "lemon-flavored Italian ice."

When dinner was finished, Julie got up from the table. "Sunday, do you want to hear my new compact discs?" she asked.

"Sure." I stood up. "Thanks for dinner, Mrs. Essentia. That was great."

"I'm glad you enjoyed it." She turned to Carl, "Carl, it's your turn to do the dishes."

"Aw, Mom!" he threw down his napkin in disgust. "How come Sunday never does them?"

Julie and I made our escape upstairs to her room before World War III erupted.

Julie's room is like an artist's studio. The sloping attic ceiling is covered with her artwork, and the shelves are stacked with art materials. We lay on the rug, listening to her discs and talking.

"I think Danny Schwartz likes me," Julie said. "He asked me out again."

"Oh, no." Carl's best friend, Danny Schwartz, was kind of a wimp.

"I told him no," Julie added, as if there was any question.

"Mmm." I started thinking about the elevator boy.

"What are you thinking about?"

"There's this boy," I told her, trying to sound casual. "I think he lives in the building. He's a musician." I cupped my chin in my hand, picturing us playing a duet together.

Julie jerked her curly head around. "You're kidding! Have you talked to him?"

"He-he saw me trying out the slide in the park. I sort of landed on his dog."

Julie laughed. "You *what?*"

I swatted her with a pillow. "You heard right."

"He must have been bowled over." Julie ducked to avoid the pillow. "Did you break his heart?"

"No. Only his dog's back was broken."

We collapsed in laughter. Every time there was any sign of letting up, Julie went into this imitation of me coming down the slide and being carried off on a dog's back. It was pretty funny.

It was so normal that I forgot all about being at Marcie's. But every once in a while, I'd remember and get a sinking feeling.

Around 10:00, Julie's mom called upstairs and said she'd drive me back to Marcie's.

My insides got crawly again the minute we hit the freeway. I was beginning to wish that I could just break my promise and stay at Julie's.

"I can't believe the bus system," I said, trying to distract myself. "This trip took five times as long by bus."

By the time we got to Marcie's front door, the spaghetti and lemon ice were threatening to make a comeback. Swallowing, I opened the

the door with my key.

"Who's there?" bellowed Winnie, coming into the hall. "Who is it?" I suppose she moved fast. For her.

Why should I answer? I live here, don't I?

She snapped on the hall light. "You frightened the living daylights out of me!" she boomed with her hand over her chest. "I thought it was an intruder."

"I'm so sorry," Mrs. Essentia apologized.

I shrugged.

"Any intruder would leave when they saw her," Julie whispered to me.

Winnie was wearing her alluring curlers and bathrobe. Winnie and Julie's mom introduced themselves.

"Sunday can come over and stay whenever she likes," Mrs. Essentia told her. "We'll take good care of her."

"As long as she lets me know," Winnie answered in a reproachful voice. "I'm too old for shocks. I've had enough to last me a lifetime."

She made such a big deal out of everything.

"Of course," said Mrs. Essentia. "Okay, Sunday?" She gave me a hug. "Take care."

"Okay. Thanks for the ride."

"You're welcome. Bye, now."

"I'll see you soon," said Julie. And they left.

Sighing, I turned and walked down the hall. I wished I had my own room to go to. Amy was asleep, clutching her owl. On her bedside table by the night-light was a package addressed to her. The return address was *The Honeymoon Cruise Ship*. There was nothing on my bed but the orange blanket.

I threw myself on it and cried. *Had Dad forgotten me?*

# *Nine*

I must have finally fallen asleep. It's easy for a person who's worn to a frazzle from skateboarding to do that. In the morning, I awoke to the sound of *Sesame Street* on the TV.

For a moment I thought that I was at home with Dad, and four years old again. It felt cozy and nice.

Then I remembered where I was. Dad was not there. He was far away on a boat somewhere. This was not my room. It was Amy's.

I wondered how I would make it through the day, and through 27 more days. I missed Dad so much. I wondered why I hadn't heard from him. I know it had been only two days since they left, but Amy had heard from him.

Suddenly, a thought hit me. I sat up and

hugged my knees. *Maybe a package had come! Maybe Winnie had it.* I rolled out of bed and padded along the hall to find Winnie.

Her door was open a crack, and I could see that she was in there, reading the newspaper. Today she was wearing a hat that looked like a bird's nest. It even had a couple of tiny birds in it. I don't know why she bothered to wear curlers at night when she squashed her hair with a hat the next day.

I tapped on the door.

"Come in!" she called from the overstuffed armchair. I went in.

I had never seen anything like Winnie's room. The floor was covered by a rug with a big rose design on it. The wallpaper even had a wild rose pattern on it, and there was a comforter with a rose design that covered the bed.

I guess Winnie likes roses.

It was so cluttered with furniture that there was hardly any room for me to walk through. I wondered how Winnie, with her huge behind, avoided knocking into things. There were lace-covered tables loaded with junk, a dresser, a china cabinet, and a bookshelf. In the middle of everything was a bed and an armchair.

The walls were covered with travel posters of England. There were lots of pictures of

Buckingham Palace, thatched cottages, and green landscapes with messages to see Britain or fly Brittania Airlines.

I just looked around the room.

Winnie chuckled. "It's quite something, isn't it?"

It sure was.

She pointed to the china cabinet. "How do you like my homage to Her Majesty?"

I squeezed past the table of framed photographs to get a closer look.

The cabinet was filled with china. And on every dish was stamped the face of a royal family member. There were miniature teapots, ashtrays, jugs, spoons, cups, and more. On every piece, grinning royalty waved.

"Um, it's—"

"I knitted seven pairs of booties when Princess Diana was having Prince William," Winnie said proudly. "I knitted one for each day of the week." I wondered whether the Prince ever wore them.

I touched a miniature thatched cottage with Prince Charles' face peeking out of a window. "I collect miniatures," I said.

"You do? Well, fancy that!"

I looked at Winnie with her newspaper spread over her lap. She sure was a character. She fit right into this room.

"My daughter used to collect miniatures when she was little," she said sadly.

I guessed that Winnie was married in the old days. "She did?"

She handed me a framed photograph from a wobbly table. "She was a lovely girl."

The picture showed a pretty, dark-haired girl standing next to Winnie in a straw hat. Winnie looked exactly the same, except she wasn't so fat.

"That picture was taken a long time ago." Winnie sounded sad.

"What happened to her?"

"She ran away when she was 16," she said abruptly. "She was boy crazy—"

"Oh." I handed her back the picture and stared at the rose-patterned rug.

There was an uncomfortable silence. Suddenly, I remembered why I was there. "Did anything come for me in the mail yesterday?" I asked.

Winnie shook her head. "Just the package for Amy came. Wait a minute." Winnie fished in her apron pocket. "The mailman left a postage due slip."

She handed me a yellow slip of paper. It was for a package addressed to me!

"Maybe there's a surprise on its way. What's your horoscope sign?"

"I'm a Taurus," I answered. I wondered if Winnie actually read those things.

She chuckled. "Taurus means that you are stubborn and bull-headed."

Stubborn! Bull-headed! I wouldn't be surprised if Winnie was a Taurus herself.

"Turn a disappointment to your advantage," she read, her fingers tracing the words.

"Okay. Well, thanks for the slip." I backed out of the room.

I couldn't wait to get out of that place! Grabbing my purse, I slipped out the front door into the sunny morning. It felt good to walk. I thought about Dad as I walked the two blocks to the post office. I was so happy thinking that I'd soon be holding his package.

There was a long line when I got to the post office. Post offices always have long lines. I read the mail fraud posters that were taped on the wall. People were getting their mail ripped open and their social security checks stolen. It sure was rough downtown. In the Tarzana post office, there were only a couple of wanted mail fraud criminals. Here there were 12.

"Next!" shouted the clerk in a shrill voice.

I went up to her window with my slip. "I need to see some identification," the clerk said.

I handed her my Luther Junior High ID card.

"The address on your ID doesn't match the slip."

"I moved," I told her. "Temporarily."

She adjusted her pointed glasses on the tip of her nose. "I'm sorry."

"But what about my package?"

"Come back with an ID showing your current address." She pointed to the slip.

"But I don't have one!" I cried.

"Sign the authorization on line four for someone else to pick it up."

"But I want my package now." My throat hurt. "Give me my package. I want my package."

"I'm sorry." She had already dismissed me and was looking at the next person in line.

I turned and ran out of the post office in tears. Everyone was against me.

Being a teenager is awful. Nobody understands.

"Hey, wait up!"

Someone was yelling at me. It was probably someone wanting to steal my postage due slip. I adjusted my backpack and ran faster.

"Wait! Wait up!"

Then I recognized the voice coming from behind me. *Oh, no.* I turned to see Eric-the-

Music-Man waving at me.

It figures. First he sees me acting like a kid, and then he sees me crying. I slowed down and scrubbed my face with my sleeve.

He ran up, panting. "Are you training for the Olympics? I've been chasing you for three blocks." He paused and clutched his side. "You left this at the post office." He held up my wallet.

"Oh, thank you." I reached for it.

He held it back with a grin. "Is this your picture?"

I snatched it away. "Yes, thank you." I even had my Snoopy barrettes on in that old picture.

He laughed. "Is your name really Sunday Moon Fairchild?"

"Yes."

"That's an interesting name."

I couldn't think of a thing to say. It was so embarrassing.

"My name's Eric Calvert."

"I know. I mean, I have to go now. I—er— have to—" I backed away.

"I have to go, too. I have cello practice."

He started walking with me.

I couldn't believe it. A boy was walking with me. And he played the cello. I tried to speak, but everything that I thought of saying to him sounded dumb to me.

*No doubt about it , Sunday, you're a genius when it comes to boys.* I'll say one thing for that moment. It was the best embarrassing moment of my life.

Finally, we reached the condo. In desperation, I spluttered out, "Er—are you a musician?"

He smiled. "I guess I am."

"Oh."

I walked into the lobby in misery. What kind of a person said *oh?*

Eric pressed the elevator button. "Which floor are you on?"

"Sixth," I said miserably.

Being alone with him in the elevator was wonderful and awful at the same time. I wanted it to go on forever, and I wanted it to stop right then.

The elevator stopped on the second floor. "I'll see you later," Eric said.

"Um—okay. Thanks for the wallet."

"You're welcome."

The elevator doors started to close. I'd miss my chance to say anything if I didn't hurry ...

"I—I play the flute," I said quickly.

He leaned his head to one side as the strip of open space narrowed. "That's interesting!" he yelled as it closed completely.

I heard him chuckle.

Winnie was right. It was a day for surprises. The biggest one was that things might improve around here.

# Ten

I couldn't wait to tell Julie that my living, breathing fantasy had talked to me. And he seemed to like it.

As soon as I got back to the condo, I went into the living room and dialed Julie's number.

"Julie, you'll never guess what happened."

"What?"

"Eric talked to me!"

"You're kidding!"

"Julie, he's so friendly. He plays the cello. He's not super cute, but he has this adorable smile and great blue eyes."

"I'm coming over!"

I squealed. "Great!"

"I want to hear every single detail. I have to get out of this house, anyway. Danny Schwartz is coming." She giggled.

"Yuck." Last year Danny had asked Julie

to the movies every time he came over to see her brother. "Get over here before he can ask you out again."

Julie laughed. "Right. Can I sleep over?"

"Sure." I hoped it would be okay with Winnie.

"Okay. Bye."

"Bye."

This day was improving by the minute. I hummed to myself on the way to the kitchen. I would soften up to Winnie and get her to let Julie sleep over. It would be a cinch.

The aroma of baking floated out of the kitchen. The smell was wonderful, but with Winnie's cooking you never knew. It was probably parrot-dropping pie.

Winnie and Amy were rolling out dough on the kitchen table. Amy was covered with flour, and Winnie's fake-fur hat had pastry sticking to it. It looked like she had white mice nesting in it.

I bit my lip and choked back a giggle. This whole thing would be ruined if I laughed. "Winnie," I started, "is it okay if Julie sleeps over? She can bring her sleeping bag."

Winnie wiped her hands on her apron. "You know I get migraine headaches." She looked at me, her face shiny red from the oven. "I can't bear noise."

"We'll be quiet, I promise."

"Well, all right then."

"Thanks, Winnie."

Amy pointed to a grubby, pear-shaped piece of dough. "Look, I made you a heart."

"Thank you." I took a breath. "And, Winnie? Will you pick up my package for me?" I showed her the slip. "The clerk wouldn't let me because my ID address was Tarzana."

Winnie straightened up. She pointed her rolling pin at me. "You can do something for me first."

"Okay."

"Watch Amy while I do the laundry."

I knew there'd be a catch. "Okay."

"Put the slip on the counter. I'll do it later."

"Thank you."

I looked at the heart. "And thanks again for the heart, Amy." I rubbed a flour smudge from her turned-up nose.

I skipped to my room. I sat on my bed and thought about Eric. I imagined him telling me that I was the girl he'd always dreamed of. I imagined that we played together in the Los Angeles Philharmonic. We were about to have our first kiss when Winnie's hat (and the flour mice) appeared around the door.

"I'm off now. If you need me, I'm in the laundry room. Get yourselves some lunch."

"Okay." My response felt automatic.

I sauntered into the kitchen, still dreaming of Eric.

Amy was sitting on her booster chair. Ollie was next to her, wearing his Snoopy bib.

"Ollie and me are hungry," Amy announced.

"Okay. I guess I could eat." I pulled open the refrigerator. "Now, let me see..."

I picked out a package of hot dogs. Thank goodness for regular, American hot dogs. They were better than Winnie's cooking any day. Amy never stopped talking while I fixed lunch.

"My favorite book is *Good night, Moon*," she said, her blue eyes fixed on me. "You say good night to all the rabbits and socks and everything. Will you read it to me? My mommy–"

"Okay. Quit talking now," I said. Then I put a row of carrot sticks onto her plate. "Eat your lunch."

Kids are funny. If you said that to an adult, they'd be insulted. But Amy just ate. Then she went right on talking.

Afterward, I went with her to our room. She opened up her toy closet. I have never seen so many toys in my life. No wonder she was spoiled.

"This is Barbie and Ken," she told me, getting out her dolls.

Dad had never bought me Barbie and Ken

dolls because he said that they were sexist. When I saw all those outfits, I understood what he meant. Amy even had a pool for Barbie to lounge by while she waited for Ken.

I looked at Barbie's curves wistfully. She sure didn't have my figure problems. I fitted a bikini over Barbie's hips. *I'd be so embarrassed if Eric could see me now,* I thought.

"How about if Barbie and Ken get married?" suggested Amy, pulling out a bride's dress. "My mommy and new daddy sent Barbie a wedding dress."

So, that was what was in the package. I breathed a sigh of relief. Dad couldn't have sent it. He'd never have chosen a wedding dress for Barbie. It must've been Marcie.

"Okay," I said.

"Barbie and Ken are going to be married just like Mommy and Daddy," said Amy.

Too bad Marcie's wedding day hadn't been just a game.

We were just sending Barbie and Ken on a skiing honeymoon when the doorbell rang.

I ran to answer it.

"Julie!" I hugged her.

"Hi. That bus is the pits."

"I know it. I'm glad you're here."

Julie walked into the living room. "Wow, this place is rich."

Amy stood in the doorway and stared at Julie.

"It looks like something in a magazine."

"I know. Er—Amy, do you want to say hi to Julie?" I prodded.

Amy shook her head.

Julie raised her eyebrows. I guess she didn't realize that Amy was shy.

"Okay, Amy," I said. "Go watch TV. I'll read that book to you at bedtime."

She looked small as she turned and ran down the hall, her pigtails bouncing.

"Come, and see my room," I said quickly. "It's awful."

"Okay."

Julie followed me down the hallway.

I pushed open the door and pointed to the owl-patterned border. "You are being watched!" I said in the scariest voice I could make.

"Yikes!" Julie exclaimed. "We need to do some artwork to cover them."

"How about writing *Tarzana High Forever* in three-foot black letters?"

Julie shook her head. "You need something colorful."

"I need someone very talented."

Julie smiled. "Now, who could that be? Come on, Sunday. Let's make a list of supplies we need and go shopping."

I gave a mock groan. "Not the lists. Please, not the lists."

Julie loved to make lists. Sometimes she made lists of the lists she had to make.

Amy wanted to come with us to the drugstore, but I told her she couldn't. We were only going for markers. Winnie was back, so I figured there was no reason that Amy should come with us.

No way was I going to share Julie, too.

But as we got out into the street, I saw Amy up at the window, waving Ollie's knitted wing at us. It made me feel mean. I waved back.

"It's wonderful getting out of that apartment," I said lifting my face to the sun. "I worry that I'm growing attached to Ollie Owl."

Julie chuckled. "Who? Whooo? Whooo?" she hooted.

I grinned. Hearing Julie's jokes felt good.

Suddenly, Julie nudged me. "Don't look now, but there's a guy coming this way."

I peeked from under a curtain of hair. I watched one boy for two whole semesters that way. Through my hair I saw Eric.

"It's him," I said to Julie.

He was wearing a yellow T-shirt that said "Musicians Have More Fun" and carrying his music case.

My heart thumped as he got closer.

"Hi," he said.

I swallowed. "Hi."

He grinned. "Are you going to the post office?"

"N-no. I mean, I am, but not now." I felt myself go red. "I'm going to the drugstore."

Eric smiled. "Well, I'll see you around." He walked on.

"Okay." My legs were shaking.

"Isn't he terrific?" I asked Julie.

"I think he likes you," Julie said.

"You do? You really do?"

"I do." She watched me as I did a side step along the curb.

Then she frowned. "Sunday, if you start dating Eric, what will I do? I wish I could find a boyfriend, too."

I turned to her. "Stop saying that."

Julie sighed. "There's just nobody interesting in Tarzana."

"There's always Dan Schwartz," I teased.

Instead of screaming "Oh, puleeze!" Julie considered the idea seriously. "Hmmm, I saw him before I left today. He's gotten contacts. He doesn't look so bad now that he's gotten rid of those dopey, bent glasses."

I couldn't believe what I was hearing. "But Julie, he's such a nerd," I said.

Julie giggled. "Well..."

I pushed open the door of the drugstore. We fooled around in the store for a while, looking for markers and poster board.

In the greetings cards section, Julie grabbed my arm. "Wait up. I want to get a birthday card."

"Who for?"

"Oh, I just like to keep one around for emergencies," she said breezily.

"Julie Essentia, you're not telling me something!" I said.

But she tried to look innocent and shook her head.

"Okay, don't tell me."

Sooner or later, she'd tell. I knew she couldn't keep it to herself forever.

I picked out a card for Dad. It had a cartoon of a cat spurting tears all over the page. It said "Being Without You Is Not Purrfect."

Julie was still looking for the right card for her mystery person, so I went over to the school supplies aisle to get some more markers. Right in front of me was a huge chalkboard made of cardboard. In big white letters it said, BACK TO SCHOOL.

Who needed reminding? Soon it was going to be registration time. I was going to have to register for L.A. High.

But I didn't want to go to L.A. High. I wanted to go to Tarzana. I wondered why I couldn't go to the school of my choice. Every day was closer to my dad's return.

But it was also closer to decision time. I wondered how I could get back home.

# *Eleven*

When we got back, everything was quiet in the apartment. I dumped the packages onto my bed. There were three markers lying there without their tops on. If they hadn't been dried out, they would have marked the yucky orange blanket.

Amy must have put them there for me.

Julie had wandered down the hall. "I don't believe this room!" she called.

"Which room?" I followed her.

She was staring into Marcie's bedroom. It looked like Marcie's style. The walls were soft gray with suede furniture and thick carpet. The bed was king-sized with a silver bedspread.

I usually avoided her room.

"It's typical of Marcie to make it look

unreal," I muttered. "Come, and look at this."
I switched on the light bulbs around Marcie's
vanity.

Julie came over. "How do I look?" She posed
like a star.

"You look fine, apart from the jeans and
shirt. Come into the closet, and I'll show you
what a true star wears."

"Wow!" Julie sucked in her breath. "Are
these all hers?"

I nodded. "They sure aren't Winnie's."

Julie giggled and walked closer to the
clothes. Everything seemed new and expen-
sive.

"Look at this fur." Julie stroked a silver fox
fur jacket.

"Huh. Just think of all the animals that were
killed to make that."

Julie shivered. "I guess you're right."

Then I caught sight of Marcie's wedding
dress. The memory of that awful day came
over me for the second time today. Marcie and
my dad were really married. There was no
going back.

All of my hatred for Marcie returned. "Go
on, Julie," I said. "Put the fur coat on."

Julie giggled. "Do you think I should?" She
slid her arms into the sleeves and snuggled
the fur to her face.

"Why not?" I took out a sequined vest and put it on. Then I picked out long, satin pants. "Look at these," I said, pulling them up over my jeans. "Don't I look great?"

"You look divine, my dear." Julie pulled off her sneakers and stepped into a pair of high heels. "Is the limo waiting?" She yanked up her jeans and tied a lace shawl over them like a skirt. "I have to get to the Oscars right away."

Pretty soon we had tried on most of Marcie's wardrobe. I didn't care that her fancy things were in a heap on the floor.

Julie frowned as she paraded up and down the room in the fur. "I don't think I'm star material," she said, picking at her teeth. "This fur keeps getting stuck in my braces."

We both broke into laughter. We fell into the heap of clothes on the floor, laughing. Every time there was any sign of quitting, Julie exposed her braces, stuck with pieces of fur, in a big smile.

We laughed so hard that we didn't hear Winnie. But she made sure we did.

She boomed, "What's going on here?"

I sat up quickly. There was an awful ripping sound from under me.

Unfortunately, Winnie noticed. "These are Miss Marcie's clothes! Take them off immediately!"

"Okay." I mumbled, pulling at the vest. "We were only playing." I groaned as some sequins came off in my hand.

Winnie's face darkened. "Be careful!"

"Okay, okay." It wasn't my fault the sequins came off so easily.

"Watch what you're doing!" Her voice rose as a couple more silver sequins shimmered to the floor. "Do you hear me?"

I think the whole building heard her.

But she wasn't going to bully me. "We heard you."

Julie scrambled to her feet and began pulling off clothes. In the jumble there was no way she could avoid stepping on clothes.

"Stop treading on those clothes!" Winnie fumed. "You teenagers have no respect!"

I glared at her. "If you'd give us a chance–"

"A chance?" She planted her hands on her hips. "It seems to me that your father's already given you too many chances. The way he raised you—"

My body shook. "I'm telling him—"

"You tell him. Tell him that if you were my daughter, I'd—"

"I'm not your daughter!" I screamed back at her. "Your daughter ran away!" Anger made me add, "And I don't blame her!"

Winnie's purple cheeks turned gray. There

was a long, ugly silence, and then she pointed to the door with a shaking arm. "Get out of here. Out! Out! OUT!"

Without another word, we scrambled to stand up in the clothes mound. I've never seen anyone that mad. Quick as a flash, we scurried to my room like a pair of frightened rabbits.

"She's really mad," Julie panted nervously when we were safely shut in my room.

"She can't talk to me that way." I pressed my back against the door as if to keep Winnie out. "Wait till I tell Dad."

Julie began to undo the buttons of Marcie's chiffon blouse with shaking fingers. "What was that about her daughter?"

I slid onto the floor and pulled off Marcie's snakeskin boots. "If she pokes her nose into my life, I'll poke my nose in hers."

"I know. But what was it about?"

Throwing the boot down, I muttered, "Her daughter ran away. Personally, I'm not surprised."

"Neither am I."

Remembering Winnie's face when I'd said that, I chewed on my lip. "I've really done it now. She had it in for me before, but now she really hates me."

Julie slumped down beside me. "You'll have

to come live at our house."

I shook my head. "I would, but Carl gives me such a hard time."

"I know, I know—" Julie rested her chin against her knee. "So, what will you do?"

I shrugged. "I'll live alone in our house, maybe. I'll breed Dobermans for protection. I'd rather have King Kong for a roommate than Winnie."

The door of Marcie's room closed with a bang.

"Teenagers," Winnie muttered as she went by. "They're nothing but trouble."

"She's an old hag," I whispered to Julie. "I'm glad I said that about her daughter."

There was a moment's silence.

Then Julie sighed. "This is turning out to be a terrible visit."

"I'm sorry. You will come again, won't you?"

Julie nodded. "If Winnie lets me. Look, let's work on the posters," she suggested. "Maybe it'll take our minds off her."

"Okay." Still shaking, I took the poster boards from the bed and set them side by side on the floor. I set out the markers and pencils. *There was no point in letting Winnie ruin my whole life,* I thought.

Together, we settled down to draw. What a relief. It was really peaceful just sketching shapes on scratch paper.

We worked silently for a while. Julie helped me design a kaleidoscope pattern for the wall next to the door. It was pretty good. She worked on an abstract design using my favorite colors—pinks and purples.

"It's beautiful," I told her. "I wish I were as talented as you."

"I'm glad you like it. And you are talented—with your flute."

"I miss practicing my flute. That old cow won't let me play it. Maybe I should take it to the park one morning."

Julie's eyes widened as she colored in. "And be arrested for impersonating the Pied Piper?"

I grinned. "I guess you're right. I don't want Eric to see me. He already thinks I do strange things in the park." I colored in a yellow triangle. "Did I tell you that Eric plays the cello?"

"Uh-huh. Maybe you should ask him if you could practice together." She leaned back and looked at her work.

"That looks great."

"It's coming along. Sun, I'm getting hungry. My mom said we could get pizza. She gave me money."

"Great. If we order pizza, then we won't

have to eat Winnie's awful food."

We crept down the hallway past Winnie's room. She didn't notice us because she was watching TV. Part of me felt sorry for Winnie, sitting alone, just staring at the TV.

The pizza parlor was three blocks away. We had to pass by L.A. High to get to the place. I avoided looking across the street, but it was impossible to miss the big sign announcing registration. I hoped I wouldn't have to go there.

At the pizza place we ordered a large pizza with everything on it.

We were just carrying it into the condo when Amy came out of the apartment next door.

"Hi," I said.

"Hi. Ollie and me have been playing," Amy told me. "Ooh, pizza. Can I have some?"

"Okay." I motioned for her to follow me. "But we have to be quiet."

Thinking it was some game, Amy crept down the hall in silence. We made it to our room without Winnie hearing us.

Julie smacked her lips. "That smells so good. I'm starved." She arranged the orange blanket and pillows on the floor so we could eat picnic style. Then she propped her finished poster next to mine.

"They look terrific, Jule. Even mine does,"

I joked. "My room is going to look great."

"Your picture is my very favorite," Amy whispered to me.

Julie smiled. "Okay. Let's eat. This is one artist who refuses to starve."

I put the pizza down and opened the steaming box. The smell of pepperoni and cheese sailed out.

"Mmmm."

"Oh, no. We forgot drinks," I wailed.

"I'm not going past Winnie's room again," said Julie. "It gives me the creeps."

"Okay, I'll go in a minute," I promised.

We sat cross-legged with paper napkins on our laps. The pizza was delicious.

"Amy, go tell Winnie that we won't be eating dinner," I said, munching on my third piece of pizza. "I don't want her getting mad at me again."

Amy got up importantly. "Okay, Sunday."

Amy came back carrying a couple of cans of root beer.

"Winnie says okay," she informed us. "She's got a headache. Here," Amy said to me. "You can have my bunny ears cup."

I mopped some melted cheese off my chin. "Thank you, Amy."

She handed Julie her drink with a shy smile.

"Thanks," Julie said, taking the cup.

I felt terrible. I wondered if I had given Winnie her headache. Maybe I shouldn't have mentioned her daughter. I drank my root beer in silence.

When we were finished eating, I balled up my paper napkin and aimed it at the trash can. Gathering up my courage, I murmured, "I think I'd better go talk with Winnie." I hated apologizing, but there was no way out. I followed the sound of the TV to her room.

I tapped on the door. There was no answer, so I banged louder.

"Come in!" Winnie called.

"It's me."

Winnie didn't answer.

"Winnie—um—I'm sorry about what I said. I didn't mean it."

She took off her glasses and rubbed them on her apron. "We both got a little heated in there." There was a silence, and then she continued, "My daughter would never have run away if we'd been a proper family." Her voice was full of emotion. "It doesn't do to raise children single-handedly."

"I didn't mean to upset you." I wanted to tell her single parenting worked all right with Dad and me, but I was through fighting.

Her flowered apron rose and settled as she sighed. "It's best forgotten."

I hung my head. "I'm sorry about Marcie's clothes, too. You won't tell her, will you?"

She clicked her tongue. "My memory's getting poor lately."

I almost hugged her. "Thank you, Winnie."

There was the beginning of a smile on Winnie's face. Putting down her knitting, she said, "So, was your horoscope right?"

I bit my lip, thinking about my package. "Well, I did have some disappointments."

She nodded. "Don't forget to turn them to your advantage."

"Okay."

"And watch out for surprises."

There were more surprises that day.

After I read *Good night, Moon* to Amy that night, she put her arms around me.

She kissed my cheek and said, "Good night, moon. Good night, Sunday Moon. Me and Ollie love you."

I didn't know what to say. I wondered how she could love me.

Finally, I just said, "Good night, Amy."

"Ollie too," Amy said.

"Okay. Good night, Ollie." I kissed them both.

I wondered if different people meant different things when they said they loved someone.

Maybe my dad didn't love Marcie as much as he loved me. But it was useless to even think it. It was like my dream of living back home—hopeless.

# Twelve

"I wish you weren't going," I moaned to Julie as we walked to the bus stop.

"I can't miss my class."

"I know."

Julie's art was as important to her as my flute was to me. But I still hated the feeling I got when she put it before me.

"Thanks for helping me decorate my room, anyway."

Julie giggled. "It looks like your room. I counted three pairs of underwear, two socks, and a piece of pepperoni under the bed."

"The pepperoni was yours."

She laughed. "Uh-oh. Here's my bus." She gave me a hug. "I'll call you when I get home."

My chest tightened. I always hated people leaving, but now it was worse. I just kept thinking about Dad leaving.

"Okay. Bye."

I waved to her as she made her way to a

seat. The driver released the brakes, and the bus gave a loud hiss as it moved away. You could tell that it was the downtown bus because of all the graffiti painted on the side. I turned and headed back to the condo. When I reached the lobby, I checked the mailbox. I felt my smile fade. As usual, there was nothing in it for me. I wondered when Winnie was going to pick up my package from Dad.

Winnie was at the hall mirror, fixing a hat with a pin. It looked like a bouquet.

"So, you're back."

"I took Julie to the bus stop."

"Humph." Her voice was reproachful. "You could have taken Amy with you."

Why should Amy share everything that was mine? It wasn't fair.

"Amy and I are off to the zoo. It's time the child had some fun," said Winnie meaningfully.

*What about me?* I thought. *Don't I deserve to have some fun?* I was expected to include Amy all the time. But they hadn't even bothered to ask me!

I marched to my room and grabbed my flute. If they could do what they liked, then I could play my flute. I crept along to the living room and opened the sliding glass doors to the balcony.

The balcony went right across the front of the building, even though the bedroom windows were too high to get to the balcony from them. How phony. I'd like to see Marcie climbing out through a window to get onto a balcony.

I thought about our yard at home. I remembered how I loved to sit in my tree house and play my flute. Marcie had no right to string it up with balloons and ribbons for the wedding. Sitting cross-legged, I rested against the railings and took my flute from its case. I put it together and placed the cool silver against my lips.

I played and played. It felt good. The anger and hurt seemed to drift away with the notes.

Suddenly, I saw someone moving between the bars of the railing. I squinted in the sunlight to the sidewalk below. Someone was waving to me.

It was Eric. *Oh, no. Every time he sees me, I'm acting weird. What kind of a person plays flutes on balconies?*

I gave an embarrassed wave. "H-hi!" Then I escaped back indoors as casually as I could.

"We're off now!" shouted Winnie as I closed the sliding glass door behind me.

"Bye, Sunday!" called Amy.

I didn't answer them. The front door

slammed shut as they left.

I stomped into the hall and kicked the hall table.

"I hate them!"

I hated myself for caring what they did. Then I saw it–a big envelope addressed to me. *My package!* Winnie didn't even tell me that she'd picked it up! It figured.

I ripped it open. It held one of Dad's rhymes and a piece of music.

*San Pedro Docks*

*Sunday Moon,*
*(Can I miss you so soon?)*

*I'm running out of time,*
*But you must have this rhyme.*

*Though hard for you, my daughter,*
*You did everything you oughta.*

*Like a trooper, you came through,*
*Despite your whole world being new.*

*I noticed all your efforts,*
*Felt proud and thankful, too.*

*So I thought I'd just remind you,*

*That I love you.*

*Dad.*

*P.S.*
*Here's music for your flute,*
*I can't wait to hear you toot.*

*Now I have to board the ship,*
*So, I leave you with Marcie's tip:*

*To Amy, be a friend,*
*And with Winnie, learn to bend.*

A tear plopped onto the page. I missed Dad and his silly rhymes so much. But why did he always mention Marcie, like they decided everything together?

I stared at the music called *Senorita Dance!* Straightening my back, I began to sight-read the music. It was a lively Spanish dance full of trills and staccatos that didn't fit my mood. As I thought of Dad, the notes trailed off into silence once more. The quiet of the apartment added to my loneliness. I wanted to talk to Dad so badly. But instead, I wrote him a postcard back.

*Dear Daddy,*

*Thank you for the music. I'll play it for you when you get back.*

*I am watching Amy, but she's gone to the zoo today with Winnie.*

*Don't you agree looking at animals in cages is a strange way to spend your time?*

*Miss you, Daddy. Come home soon.*

*Love,*
*Sunday*

I wandered around the apartment and thought to myself, *this is what my life would be like if I stayed here. Miserable.*

I scanned the bookshelves, but Marcie didn't have any good novels to read. She did have plenty of books on self-improvement.

There were also piles of magazines. I flipped through them. There was a whole fashion spread on school clothes for the fall semester.

Where would I be this fall?

I flipped through the pages to an article about makeup.

*Is your complexion Dry/Oily/Combination?* the article asked.

I went into Marcie's bathroom to examine my skin (the article said is was important to have proper lighting). I looked terrible.

117

Usually my face is even-colored but now it was blotchy and pale. And there was a volcano erupting on my forehead to prove it. Great!

I rubbed at the pimple and made it a worse mess than ever. Now I had a pimple and a huge red splotch across half of my forehead. I might as well draw an arrow pointing straight to it.

Just then the front doorbell rang. Uh-oh. No one was going to see me this way.

I looked through the peep hole. "Who is it?"

"Eric. Eric Calvert."

Eric!

"Uh, hello. I mean, hi."

"I thought maybe you'd like to come downstairs," he said. "There's only Mom and me. And she's busy in her study."

"Oh."

There was a long silence as my brain scanned possible replies. "So will you come?" Eric asked.

"Uh. Sure," I croaked. "I mean, yes. I'll be right there."

"Great." I heard him whistle as he went downstairs. "I'll see you there."

I dashed back to the bathroom.

My mind was doing flip-flops. Eric Calvert had asked me to his apartment!

But my pimple!

Maybe I should tell him I have a contagious disease. We could have this wonderful relationship through his front door.

Maybe if I tied a scarf over my forehead, I could hide it.

I ran into Marcie's room and went through her scarves. I didn't care what Winnie thought. It was a matter of life and romance. In a panic, I ended up with a purple scarf with Indian bells sewn around the edge. I tied it low on my forehead and went downstairs.

I pressed Eric's doorbell, my heart thudding through my whole body.

Eric opened the door and Dandy leapt on me, barking like a maniac.

"Get down, Dandy. Sit. Sit!"

I kept the smile I'd practiced upstairs.

"Come in," Eric said, staring at my headdress. "He won't bite."

"Um, this is the latest fashion. The gypsy look." I always babble when I'm really nervous.

He laughed. "It is?"

"Absolutely." To cover my shyness, I joked, "Cross my palm with silver."

He grinned. "Come in, come in. I knew you had a sense of humor when I saw you coming down that slide."

I felt my cheeks burn at the memory of that.

But before I had a chance to say anything, he ushered me into the living room. I looked around, pretending to be relaxed.

"Here." Eric moved a pile of music off of a chair. "Do you want to sit down?"

I perched on the edge. "Thanks."

"Do you like lemonade?"

"Sure."

Eric rushed into the kitchen, and Dandy leapt after him. I went over to the shiny grand piano by the window and fingered the keys softly.

"Do you play?" asked Eric, coming in with the lemonade.

"No," I said. "I play the flute."

"I remember," said Eric. He put his head to one side the way he had that time at the elevator. "That's very interesting."

We both laughed.

"My mother composes music for the piano. She's working in her study."

"What about your dad?"

"He's dead," he said, sitting down.

I bent to stroke Dandy's head. "I didn't mean—"

"Hey, how about some music?" Eric broke in.

He jumped up from his seat and went over to the stereo. Loud crashing sounds began.

The noise was tremendous.

"Can't we have something peaceful?" I shouted.

Eric gave a maestro's bow and turned off the stereo. "Sorry, Shostokovitch is like that."

"Shosta who?"

He grinned. "I'm just showing off my expert knowledge."

I smiled back. He really was nice.

Nothing got in our way after that. We talked as if we'd known each other a long time. He was so easy to talk to. He was the kind of guy I knew existed, despite the Carl Essentia types. We had so much in common.

He told me about the L.A. Conservatory of Music. He went there every day during the summer. "I like the studying," he said. "It's just that I never get to talk to anyone. Everyone just goes to the practice rooms."

"What about lunch time?"

"Most people go home. I guess musicians aren't very social."

"I think they're great," I said. Oops—how could I say something like that? I could feel myself blush.

Now I'd used up all my courage. I had none left to ask Eric if musicians went to L.A. High.

But it didn't matter. I was determined I was going to Tarzana.

# *Thirteen*

I called Julie the next day and told her about my wonderful afternoon with Eric. She was impressed, but for the first time, she seemed reluctant to come see me.

"Julie, please come over here," I begged. "Winnie won't be here if that's what's worrying you. She's going out."

"Why can't you come here?"

"Because I have to baby-sit Amy. Come on. It's Saturday night."

Julie sighed. "Okay. But there's just one problem."

"What problem?" I asked.

"I promised I'd see Danny tonight."

"Danny!" So, Julie was holding out on me. "Is this like a date or what?"

"Well—no—not exactly." Julie giggled. "He's coming over to see Carl."

"I don't get it."

"Well, we sort of told each other maybe we'd go out sometime," Julie admitted.

"Julie!"

"He's really different this summer, Sunday. You'll see."

"Really?" I hoped he'd changed from the days when he wore bent glasses and talked about math all the time.

"Hey, why don't I bring him over?"

I sighed. "Okay. Bring Dan."

First I share my dad, then my room. Now I was going to have to share Julie with Dan Schwartz!

"Sunday, you're the best friend! I'll have to bring Carl, too. Otherwise, Mom will—"

"Carl!" Saturday nights with me sure must be boring if Julie resorted to Carl. I sighed heavily. "Okay. Carl, too."

Then I had a great idea. If Julie was bringing Dan and Carl, I could invite Eric! It could be a mini party!

I squeezed the receiver with excitement. "Julie, I just thought of something terrific. How about if I invite Eric? We could make popcorn and...."

"Great! I'll bring some of my mom's cookies."

I squealed with excitement. "I'll make some lemonade!" I hoped Eric could come!

"Don't get here till after seven." I told Julie. "Winnie'll be gone by then. She would go crazy if she thought I was having boys over."

The doorbell rang at 7:30. I put the chips and guacamole dip on the coffee table and took a deep breath. I opened the door. It was Julie, Dan, and Carl.

"Hi."

"Hi," Julie said with a pleased smile.

Carl walked in without speaking. He jammed his hands into his pockets, strolled to the white couch, and plopped down.

"What a place!" he said, whistling.

"It's pretty snazzy," agreed Dan.

"Doesn't he look better with his contacts?" Julie whispered to me while Dan inspected the living room.

"I guess." I had to admit Dan looked better without glasses, but I still couldn't figure it out. Dan was not Julie's type.

"Do you have any video games?" demanded Carl, loudly.

I shook my head.

"I brought Scrabble. How about a game?" suggested Julie.

"Nah," said Carl. He pretended to throw an imaginary baseball at me. "That's boring."

"Um." I stuck my thumbs into the back of my jeans waistband. "I don't know if there are any cards around here."

Julie stepped nearer to Dan. "Let's play Scrabble. What do you say, Danny?" She smiled sweetly.

I'd never seen her act that way before.

Dan smiled back. "Okay, Jule."

I couldn't believe Dan called her Jule. Jule was my name for Julie!

For once I was glad to have Amy interrupt things for me. "Sunday! Sunday! I'm through in the tub!" she called.

Everyone looked at me.

"Um, I have to go get Amy to bed. You guys set up the board."

I went to the bathroom tense with nerves. It was 7:35, and Eric wasn't here yet. Maybe he wasn't coming. He said he would, but maybe he changed his mind.

Maybe he got sick!

Amy was sitting in the tub, waiting for me. I grabbed her and swung her around, and then wrapped her up in the towel.

"Sunday, swing me again. Please?"

"No," I told her rubbing her little back. "Not tonight. I'll swing you more tomorrow, okay?"

"Do you promise?" Amy knew how to get her way with me.

"I promise. Here, let me dry your hair."

I loved the smell of Amy's shampoo. It

reminded me of bath times with Dad when I was little.

"Who's here?" she asked as I brushed her damp hair.

"It's just Julie. Okay, get into your pajamas."

I got her to bed and read her *Good night, Moon* as usual. But tonight all I could think of was Eric coming.

It was past 8:00 by the time Amy was drifting off to sleep, and Eric still hadn't come.

"Good night, Amy."

"Good night, Sunday," she murmured sleepily.

I kissed her cheek. She smelled wonderful.

The doorbell rang, and my heart started pounding. I went into the living room and opened the door.

"Hi."

"Hi, Eric. Come, and meet my friends." Eric looked great in white pants and a surfer shirt.

"We're in here, Sunday!" called Julie from the dining room.

"Oh, you're in here..."

"The table's better. It's okay, isn't it?"

"I guess." I hadn't spent much time in Marcie's dining room before. It felt kind of like forbidden territory. The dining room table is made of this black, shiny stuff, and there's an artificial centerpiece in the middle of it. It just didn't seem like a comfortable place to eat—or play Scrabble. "Uh," I began, "Eric, this is Julie. Dan, Carl, guys, this is Eric."

Dan stood up like an adult and said, "Hi, there!"

Carl greeted Eric in a real loud voice.

Julie just smiled and said, "We've already met."

Eric gave one of his winning smiles and said, "Hi, everyone."

"Er, how about something to drink everyone?"

Julie and Dan nodded their heads, but Carl just sat there. I went to the black, polished cabinet beside the dining room table to get some glasses. It felt weird to have all these people here, and the atmosphere wasn't helping. Everybody seemed really tense. There weren't any regular glasses in the cabinet. There were only the crystal ones. Oh, well, I thought to myself. This was a special occasion after all! I got everyone some root beer, and then I sat down at the table.

"That light is way too bright," Julie said, pointing to the chandelier. It makes this place look like an operating room.

Dan jumped up and dimmed the lights. "It's more romantic this way," he said.

Personally, I thought it was spooky the way our faces reflected in the black polished table. It felt peculiar for the five of us to be sitting here in Marcie's formal dining room, playing Scrabble.

We each picked a tile to see who started and Carl got the *A*.

"The best man always wins," he said looking sideways at Eric.

"Here, Sunday," Eric said. "You choose next." His hand brushed mine as he passed me the box. Wow! The air was electric with excitement. I think it was mostly mine.

Carl spread out his tiles to spell *haunt*. "Whooooo hoooo!" he hooted loudly in my ear.

"Ssh. You'll wake my..."

"Well, excuse me!" he cried in a stage whisper.

The air bristled. Julie hurried to put down her letters to spell *guest*.

It was Dan's turn. He took forever, finally adding *s* to *haunt* and added *pook* to spell *spook*.

"How's that?" he asked.

"That's great, Dan," Julie murmured admiringly. "It's good when words fit."

"Spooks haunt guest. Spooks haunt guests," intoned Carl. "Come to think of it, it is kind of creepy around here."

"Don't say that, Carl. I keep hearing noises. I'm scared enough as it is."

"It's only the other people in the building," I sounded more confident than I felt. Taking a breath, I said. "It's my turn. I can't think of any more ghost words." I put down the tiles to spell *girl*.

Eric chuckled. "Thanks, I need that!" he said and put down the tiles under my girl to spell *love*.

My heart leapt. Was there a message here? There was a moment's stillness. Then, in a sudden movement, Carl reached over and grabbed the box of tiles, sending Eric's glass flying. There was a shattering crash of glass. Eric jumped up as root beer spread on his white pants.

"What in the world is going on here?"

Julie shrieked. A huge dark shape stood silhouetted against the light.

"A ghost!" yelped Carl.

"With two heads..." Dan whispered.

The shadow was eerie. It looked like a ghost with exploded brains.

But I knew better. After all, what self-respecting ghost would wear a hat shaped like a volcanic eruption?

"What are you kids doing here? Who gave you permission to be here?" yelled Winnie.

My guests scrambled to their feet.

"We're sorry—we—" began Eric.

"Sorry, my foot! What are you doing, scratching up Mrs. Fairchild's best polished table?"

"Come on. We'd better leave," said Dan.

Julie looked at me.

"Sunday, do you want me to stay?" asked Eric, not moving.

Tears of shame burned in the back of my eyes. "No. No thank you, Eric. Please, everyone. Just go."

"I'll call you tomorrow," whispered Julie as she hurried after Dan and Carl.

As I closed the door, Winnie muttered, "Teenagers. You're all boy crazy." I was sick and tired of the way she lumped all teenagers together.

"I'm not boy crazy!" I retorted.

"What do you call inviting three boys over the minute my back is turned?" Winnie asked.

I wanted to cry. "They're my friends—my friends—"

"You're supposed to be baby-sitting Amy."

"I am baby-sitting! Amy's in bed!" I screamed.

"Don't you yell at me!"

Just then there was the padding of pajama feet. "I woke up," Amy whimpered from the doorway, rubbing her eyes.

"Now see what you've done!" accused Winnie. "Come on, Amy. Winnie will get you some warm milk."

"You—you can't treat me this way," I whispered fiercely as she pushed by me. "I'm calling my dad!"

"No, you aren't. You get to bed!"

Dad had given me a telephone number to contact the ship. It was only to be used in an emergency, he'd said. Well, this was an emergency.

While Winnie and Amy were in the kitchen, I went to my room and searched for the number. When I found it, I carried Amy's Mickey Mouse telephone under the orange blanket.

My heart did strange things as I dialed the long set of numbers Dad had given me. At last, the operator came on the line.

"Operator, I'd like to make a person-to-person call to Mr. Joseph Fairchild." My voice trembled.

Gulping on tears, I waited. I wanted my voice to be clear for this.

There were lots of clicks and buzzes coming

through static. After a long while, from far away, came the sound of a phone ringing.

"I have a person-to-person call for Mr. Joseph Fairchild," said the operator.

"Hold the line please, caller," she said to me.

"Okay." Soon I would hear Dad's voice. I couldn't wait.

There was a click. Then far, far away a distant voice muttered, "Hello?"

It was him!

"Daddy! Daddy!"

"Sunday! Honey, is that you? Is everything okay?"

I could just about hear his wonderful voice. It was great.

"What is it, sweetheart?"

Suddenly, I forgot everything I'd planned to say. The whole misery of being so far from him overwhelmed me. I started to cry.

"I want you here, Daddy. I just want you h-home—"

"I can't hear you, honey. It's the middle of the night here. Are you sure you're all right?" His voice kept fading and returning like someone playing with the volume.

"Come home." I was sobbing. "Daddy, I need you."

The line crackled. "How is Amy? Are you

taking good care of her—?"

That came through clear enough.

"Daddy, forget Amy for a minute. I have something important to tell you. Daddy, I need—"

"Terrible line—I love you, honey—"

I sobbed. "I l-love you, too!"

Pleep. Plop.

It sounded like the receiver had been dropped into the sea. We'd been cut off.

I threw down the phone and buried my face in the pillow.

"Daddy, Daddy, where are you?" I sobbed. "I can't do it, Daddy. I can't do it alone—" I wept.

Suddenly I felt skinny legs crawl onto the bed beside me. A soft, furry nose tickled my cheek.

"Ollie will kiss it and make it better," whispered Amy. She wiggled her warm little body into my back.

I turned and cried into her hair. "Oh, Amy. Oh, Daddy. I want to go home."

# Fourteen

We slept that way all night.

"Amy," I whispered the moment she woke the next morning. "Do you want to come to the the mall with me?"

She nodded sleepily. "Can we go to the pet shop?"

"Sure."

Later, in the pet shop, she was in heaven. "Oh, she's so cute," she cooed, stroking a tiny kitten. "Can we have her?"

I petted the kitten. "I'm sorry, Amy. We have to ask—your mom and my dad."

Amy pouted. "But Mommy and Daddy are on a boat."

I guess I was getting used to her calling my dad "Daddy." For the first time it didn't hurt when she said that.

"You'll have to wait till they get back."

Amy never stayed mad for long. She giggled

as a tiny pink tongue started to lick her fingers. "It tickles."

I put my hand out. The tongue felt like a small piece of sandpaper.

"You sure are pretty," I told the baby kitten.

The kitten purred. It was too young to be without its mother. I guess it was like Amy. I remembered how she'd screamed when her mother left.

When Amy had petted everything twice, we left the pet shop and headed down the mall.

The downtown mall was nothing like the one in the valley. There were no Luther Junior High kids racing around. And everyone looked rich. You'd think there was no poverty in L.A.

We stopped to look in the window of a gift shop. It was called *Bear Facts*.

"Can we go in? Can we? Can we?" begged Amy. Her ponytail bounced as she jumped.

"Okay," I said.

I had never seen so many bears in so many different ways. There were stuffed bears riding bikes, satin bears swinging from trapezes, and even bears dressed in tutus dancing on pointed ballet slippers. There were bear cups, bear stationery, and even bear clocks.

I ended up using my second and third week

allowances to buy Amy and me matching T-shirts. On the front of the T-shirts was the California state flag, a big brown bear. Underneath the flag, it said, "Welcome to L.A."

When I gave Amy hers, she put her arms around my neck. "Now we're really twins," she said.

I hugged her back. It was kind of nice that we had the same coloring.

I looked at my watch. "It's almost noon. Let's go."

Julie had called me early that morning and arranged for Carl, Dan, and herself to meet me at the indoor ice rink. She said she'd try to reach Eric, too. I hoped she had.

Amy held onto my hand as we walked toward the rink.

I could see Julie and Dan waiting inside. Then my heart jumped as I saw Eric standing next to them.

"Hi!" I said, happily. "This sure was a great idea." It felt good knowing I had such great friends.

"We planned it last night outside your apartment," said Dan.

I giggled. "Did you really think she was a ghost?"

"I sure did," said Dan.

We broke into laughing.

Fortunately, Amy was showing Ollie the skaters through the glass window. I'm not sure she'd like to hear us laughing at Winnie.

"Let's go rent our skates," Eric said.

As I was tying Amy's skates, I whispered to Julie, "Where's Carl? Is this your date with Dan?"

Julie shook her head. "Carl didn't want to come because of Eric."

"Eric? How come?"

"Carl *likes* you," she whispered.

"Likes me? As in boy-girl likes?"

"Uh-huh."

"You've got to be kidding!" I gasped. "I never thought he liked me. He should be nicer to people."

"I don't think he knows how."

There wasn't time to say any more, because Eric and Dan came over wearing their skates.

Eric didn't look balanced.

"I'm warning you. I'm totally uncoordinated," he said as we wobbled on our blades.

"I am, too." It was the perfect excuse to clutch his arm.

"Look at Amy!" Julie gasped.

Amy had taken off and was doing some expert twirls.

"She's had lessons since she was two," I explained.

"It's like riding a bike," said Dan, edging away from the bar. "It's easy when you know how."

"And it's impossible when you don't!" yelped Eric as his arm pulled away from my hand, and he hit the ice.

He dragged himself up and moved forward unsteadily. In a second, he was down again, landing on his foot.

"I liked that foot," he moaned. "We went everywhere together."

I tried to pull him up and fell down myself. "Ouch!" I howled. "That hurt."

Eric tried to help me and fell down again. "Let's do this again someday."

I laughed.

"Let's try it together," Julie offered, circling us.

Dan skated over confidently. "Let's go. Let's go."

We linked arms. I thought two against two were fair odds. But Eric and I had gravity on our side. In half an hour, the four of us had scraped, hit, or slid on every part of our bodies.

The humiliating part was that Amy kept skating by and offering to help.

When we landed in a heap for the hundredth time, Dan muttered, "I quit. My leg has gone numb. I can't skate any longer."

"Dan," said Eric calmly. "That's *my* leg."

We collapsed with laughter.

"I'm weak from hunger," Julie finally complained.

We agreed food was a good idea. With sore ankles we limped to the rink's coffee shop.

"Can I have a hamburger?" asked Amy, dancing around on her uninjured feet.

"Sure," Julie told her. "I think you deserve a medal."

I giggled.

It was the most wonderful afternoon all summer. And when Eric and I rode home on the bus with Amy, it was perfect.

"Do you want to go see a movie tomorrow afternoon?" asked Eric as we said good-bye in the elevator. "There's a two dollar special before five."

"Yes," I said. *Yes, yes, yes.*

If my dad had been home, it would've been the best afternoon of my life.

# Fifteen

After that wonderful afternoon, Amy and I went to bed early, happy but exhausted.

The next morning, the telephone rang. I picked up the receiver. "Hello?"

The operator's voice came through, "I have a person-to-person call for Sunday Moon Fairchild."

My heart leapt. "Yes. I mean, that's me!"

"Go ahead, caller."

From far away came a clear voice. "Sunday, honey, is that you?"

"Daddy! Daddy!"

I heard him laugh. "I've been trying to reach you since your call. Is everything all right? Honey, how are you doing?"

"Okay, I guess. Oh, Daddy, it's great to hear your voice."

"It's wonderful to hear yours, too, sweetheart."

"Daddy, guess what?"

"What?"

"I met this neat boy who lives in the building."

Dad chuckled. "You did? What's he like?"

I sighed. "He's really neat, Dad. He plays the cello, and his name's Eric. He's 16. Is it okay if I go to a movie with him?"

"Hmm." Dad seemed to consider for a moment.

"I'll take Amy with me."

"What does Winnie think of him?"

I made a noise. "Winnie—she worries too much. The only boyfriend she would approve of is Prince Charles."

Dad laughed. "But he's married."

"Exactly."

Dad enjoyed that one. When he'd gotten his voice back he said, "Well, I guess you can go if the movie's all right for a four-year-old. If you say this boy is okay, then I believe you."

"He is, Dad. Thanks."

"So, Sunday, is Winnie taking good care of you both?" Dad asked.

"I guess so. She's pretty hard to get along with," I answered.

"What's that?" His voice faded.

I shouted loudly into the phone, "I said, Winnie is hard to get along with!"

"Sweetheart, I hope you're making an effort—" he shouted back.

"Sure, Dad. I'm being your model daughter."

"Okay, sweetheart. This call is going to clean me out. There's a letter on its way telling you about the cruise."

The cruise. I felt the familiar stab of jealousy. But I didn't let it ruin the call.

"Is the cruise fun?" I asked.

"It's great. I feel like a kid again," Dad answered.

"Hey, I'm the kid, remember?"

"Are you sure?"

"Oh, Daddy."

I said good-bye, and then I danced into the kitchen to get Amy to talk to her mom.

She rushed to the phone, calling "Mommy! Mommy!"

Winnie looked up at me. She was sitting at the table with her hands on her hips wearing her bird-nest hat. I'd seen that hurt expression on her face once before.

"So, I'm hard to get along with, am I?"

"Well, I—um—"

Stirring her tea, she said, "My daughter said the same thing at your age."

"She did?" I was relieved that she wasn't mad. But I felt bad that I'd upset her again.

Winnie poured another cup of tea. Without asking, she pushed it across the table.

"My daughter was everything to me," Winnie said. "When she left, my world was over." Her glasses were fogged up, so I couldn't see her eyes. But I think she was crying.

"I should have made my own life, like your father and Miss Marcie are doing. But I devoted myself to her."

As I watched Winnie take off her glasses and rub them on her apron, I think I understood. She didn't want me to spoil Dad and Marcie's life together. She didn't know me. I would never do that to my dad.

Amy ran in just then. "Mommy and Daddy are coming home soon!" she announced happily.

I smiled at her. "I know." There were only a couple of weeks left until they returned.

Things were looking better. Dad would be home soon, and I had a date with Eric.

\*     \*     \*     \*     \*

As I sat next to Eric in the theater, I couldn't help feeling terrific. I was on a date with the greatest guy in the world! Who cared if we were chaperoned by Amy and Ollie?

The movie was a science fiction story about aliens invading Earth. It was pretty dumb. There was a lot of shooting and killing.

"These things make me nervous," I whispered to Eric. "I hope it doesn't give Amy nightmares."

"Amy's fine." He put his arm around my shoulders. "Don't be nervous," he whispered.

We turned back to the screen and pretended to be interested in who was winning. I guess it was the humans, because the music was rising in a triumphant crescendo. As the movie came to an end, Eric kept his arm around me.

It was the best movie I have ever gone to.

After the movie, we got hamburgers at a fast-food place. It was great waiting in line with Eric, even if I was holding hands with Amy instead of him.

"That'll be $6.50," said the cashier.

I felt embarrassed. Maybe Eric didn't have enough money to pay for this.

"Let me get ours," I said, opening my purse.

"I have a quarter," said Amy in a high-pitched voice.

"It's okay, Amy," Eric told her.

Then he held his hand over mine. "It's my treat. My mom gave me extra money."

I left his hand there and smiled. "Thank

you, Eric." Amy smiled, too.

"That'll be $6.50," repeated the cashier.

"I'm sorry," Eric said. Then we looked around and saw that everyone in line had been waiting for us.

That was embarrassing. But it was worth it.

Later, outside my front door, Eric held me back as Amy ran in.

"Wait up a second," he said. I closed the door behind me.

"Will you meet me in the park tomorrow morning at 7:00?"

"Okay." I smiled.

"Sunday, will you move away when your dad gets back from his cruise?" he asked seriously.

I swallowed. "I don't know. We need a bigger place. I'm used to having my own room."

"I hope you stay here," Eric said.

It felt good to hear him say that. But the mention of the future, as always, made me queasy.

"Eric, I don't know where I'll be living, what school I'll be going to, how I'll get along with Marcie—" There was a hard lump in my throat.

"How come?"

I swallowed. "See, Marcie and I don't get

146

along. I—I did some pretty mean things to her before she left."

Eric looked at me. "I get it. You didn't want her to marry your dad?"

"I didn't want anyone to marry him."

He was quiet for a minute. "Do you know what? I've wanted my mom to remarry ever since my dad died. I wished for a family. But," he said, "I guess you can't choose the family you want."

"No," I agreed. "You're stuck with them."

There was a silence as we both thought about what all this meant. Then Eric sighed. "Sunday, do you feel like you're all alone sometimes?"

I nodded. He understood.

"Does it feel like it's everyone else and just you?"

He felt the same way. "Yes. But I do have my dad. He's terrific."

"How about Amy?"

"She's okay," I admitted.

He smiled. "And Winnie—what about her?"

I giggled. "She's semi-okay—"

"And Dandy?"

He went on adding more and more ridiculous names to the list. He asked if I liked the alien space invaders, the cashier at the restaurant, Ollie Owl.

I laughed. Suddenly, the whole world was okay with me, even though the future was still dark and unknown.

# *Sixteen*

"Hurry with your breakfast," I told Amy the next morning. "We're going to the park."

Winnie slapped a bowl of something in front of me. "It's a bit early for the park, isn't it?" She held her forehead with the back of her hand.

I prodded the lumps in my bowl. "We want to go before it gets too hot. Isn't that right, Amy?"

Amy nodded. "That's right."

"I don't know," muttered Winnie, "why you want to rush off to the park, just when I'm coming down with one of my migraines."

"We'll keep out of your way so that you can rest."

Winnie touched her temples with her fingertips. "I suppose it's all right. My head's bursting."

"I'll get you your pills." I ran to her room and got her pills from her dresser. I'd seen her take them before.

Winnie took them with a weak smile. "Thank you. Teenagers," she clucked. "There's no telling what you'll do next."

Then I was going to eat Winnie's oatmeal. Winnie's burnt oatmeal. I'd eat 10 plates of it if it meant that I could go meet Eric.

Winnie dried her hands on her apron. "Just make sure you watch Amy. I don't want you two talking to strangers."

"I'll watch her."

I rinsed off my bowl and stacked it in the dishwasher. After that breakfast, rattlesnake stew or boiled sheep's eyes would be gourmet delights.

"Hurry up, Amy. We don't want to be late."

What if I was too late? Eric gave Dandy a run every morning, but what if today Dandy was tired? I pulled nervously on my shirt.

Amy headed for the swings as I scanned the park for Eric's blue running suit. Maybe he was avoiding me.

I slumped onto the bench and started counting my misfortunes. Absent Father, Witch Stepmother, Moving.

I was just up to number four, Flat Chest, when four giant paws landed on me. It was

Dandy, and he slobbered all over me with his long purple tongue.

"Dandy, Dandy!" I stroked his fur.

"Dandy, get down." Eric ran up, grinning. "I think he likes you."

"I think you're right," I said, ducking Dandy's licks.

Eric sat next to me. "Throw him something," he said, rubbing Dandy's head. "He'll chase anything."

I picked up a stick and threw.

Dandy bounded after it, with his ears flapping and his tail wagging.

"He's a great dog."

Eric grinned. "He's dumb, but friendly."

We both watched Dandy. Soon he came bounding back, carrying something in his mouth.

"Give it here, boy. Give it here," said Eric, tugging at the thing hanging from his jaws.

I saw then that it was a glove with the fingers sticking out of Dandy's mouth.

I giggled. "They look like teeth hanging that way."

"Maybe your name should be Goofy," Eric said to Dandy. Dandy just barked back. Neither of us could stop laughing. Dandy looked so funny jumping up and down with the fingers flapping in his jaw.

It wasn't until I noticed that the swings were empty that I felt the warmth drain from me.

"Eric? Have you seen Amy? She's not at the swings."

"Your sister? No—"

It didn't matter that he had just called Amy my sister. The important thing was to find her. "I think she's lost," I said.

"You search over there," Eric pointed to the duck pond, "and I'll go over by the rock path."

"Okay."

Eric and Dandy ran off over the grass as I hurried towards the duck pond.

What if she were really lost? For good? I'd promised my dad I'd take care of her, and I hadn't.

I ran toward the nearby bushes. "Amy!" My heart beat faster. "Amy!"

I searched behind the bushes. But there was nothing but a bare mound of grass. Where was that kid? She promised to stick by me, and she hadn't. When I found her, I'd—I'd—

Suddenly, I stopped. I remembered the posters of the missing kids. What if Amy had been kidnapped?

My stomach lurched. This was terrible. "Amy! Amy!" Please don't let it be true.

I pictured her being carried off by a stranger, screaming and kicking. It would be my fault if she were lost forever.

I sprinted back to the park entrance. My heart jumped as I saw some kids playing by the gate. But Amy wasn't one of them. Where was she?

"Amy!" I ran to the pond. It looked still and peaceful. Could Amy have drowned? Could smooth waters cover her as if nothing was down there?

There was an old man feeding the ducks.

I ran up to him. "Did you see a little girl with blond pigtails?" I panted.

He scratched his unshaven chin. "Well, now. Can't say I—"

"Thanks. Thank you—"

I ran over to a clump of trees. Please let her be there. Please let her be there.

But she wasn't there either. My legs felt numb. The shadows from the trees were not hiding Amy. She was gone. I felt sick.

Then it hit me!

I didn't want her to be gone.

It was true. When she'd hung around asking me to talk to Ollie, interrupting my time with Julie, I'd wanted her to get lost. But when I played with her and read her stories, she'd sneaked her way into my heart.

She was really a great kid. And I wanted her back more than anything.

Skirting the far side of the park, I looked behind the restrooms, under the benches. Despairingly, I even looked in the trash can. What if I found her little body in its pink overalls? But, thankfully, I didn't. She wasn't in there.

Was she somewhere else, hurt, crumpled, calling for me?

Tears were running down my cheeks, but I didn't care. Amy, Amy, oh, Amy....Where are you?

Suddenly, I saw something move ahead. My heart squeezed, and then stopped beating as a tip of blue appeared. Amy's blue ribbon! A little yellow head, attached to that blue ribbon, peeked out from behind a tree.

Relief and joy shot through me.

Amy!

My heart beat again. And right then I knew that I loved her. I really loved that kid.

"Amy! Amy!" I screamed, running toward her.

She looked up. "Hi."

I fell on my knees beside her. "What are you doing?"

"Ollie wanted to bury nuts," she told me innocently.

"Oh, Amy!" I cried, hugging her to me. "I thought you were lost. I was so scared."

She squeezed her little arms around my neck. "I wasn't lost."

"Tell me the next time you go off like that, okay?"

"Okay, Sunday."

Taking her little hand in mine, I felt weak. "Come on. Eric is looking for you, too."

\* \* \* \* \*

I was glad Dad wasn't around to hear about me losing Amy. His phone call seemed a long time ago. So much had happened since then. I sat on my bed that afternoon re-reading a letter from him I'd gotten that day. It sounded like he was having a great time on the cruise. Knowing that didn't make me feel as bad as it used to.

I guess having fun of my own helped.

But how would it feel when Dad and Marcie were back? Would the same pain be there whenever I had to share Dad with Marcie? I sighed. Maybe now that they were married, they wouldn't kiss in front of me. That would be a start.

Eric had suggested that I try to act friendly around Marcie. He said that maybe she'd mellow out. He'd talked to her in the elevator lots of times, and she seemed okay, he'd said. I'd told him that he didn't know her like I did. He said he guessed not.

Eric was great to talk to about feelings. He was the most understanding boy I'd ever known.

We planned to meet in the park again today. I would tell him about my letter. I lay back on my bed, thinking about how much I liked him. I couldn't wait for Dad to meet him.

Suddenly, the door burst open, interrupting my thoughts. Winnie stomped in without knocking.

"What's this I hear about meeting boys in the park?" she demanded.

I jumped. "What? Would you please knock?"

Winnie ignored me. "You've been meeting boys in the park."

"I—I don't know what you mean."

"Don't play dumb with me, girl. You've been meeting boys."

"I have not been meeting boys ." She made it sound like a whole army.

But it was hopeless trying to reason with her when she was angry. She pointed a finger at me. "You've been talking to strangers."

I sat up, mad as anything. "I have not!"

"You meet boys in the park."

"I don't meet boys." My face throbbed. "It's just one boy."

"I knew it!" she cried triumphantly, folding her arms across her chest.

I glared at her. "So what if I meet a boy?"

There were two angry red spots on Winnie's cheeks. "So what? You lose Amy, that's what!"

Groan. That was it. "Amy should've stuck by me. She—"

"Amy is four years old!" Winnie yelled. "You are 14!"

"It wasn't my fault. She—"

"You ought to know better. I told Mrs. Fairchild that teenagers are trouble. 'Don't leave me with a teenager,' I said. They're all trouble."

I shouted, "I'm telling my father!"

"Your father gave me full responsibility!"

I shook all over. "You've got no right—"

"While I'm in charge, there will be no meetings with boys in parks."

"You won't stop me!"

"We'll see about that! Who is this boy, anyway?"

Hot tears welled up like a pain. "It's none of your business."

"Fine, then. You can stay in your room until you're ready to tell me."

"I will not! You can't keep me prisoner!"

"We'll see about that, Miss Teenager. I'll be in the kitchen across the hall. You'd better not leave this room for anything."

And before I knew it, she had slammed the door.

I flung myself onto my bed. Tears of anger welled up inside me. Daddy, why did you leave me here?

Eric would be at the park in the morning, waiting. He'd think I had forgotten.

Or, he'd think that I didn't care. My one big chance with a boy was ruined. I'll bet Winnie never had a boyfriend. Winnie was never 14.

I cried forever. If only I could get a message to him. I sat up, sobs still shaking my body.

Maybe if I made a big sign—

I peeled off my kaleidoscope poster from the wall. Then, using my markers, I wrote on the back in big letters: ERIC. CAN'T MAKE PARK. SUNDAY.

I stood on Amy's bed and taped it to the window. Just below was the balcony. The balcony!

If I got out onto it here, I could creep along to the part outside the sliding glass doors. The little separating wall would be a breeze to climb over. I could get through into the living room and escape out the front door.

Could I do it? I opened the window and

looked out. The drop from the window to the balcony was about three feet. But underneath it was six floors of space.

I pulled myself up to the windowsill. Remembering my flute, I jumped back onto the bed. I gathered it with some music, my door key, and wallet. Then, stuffing everything into my backpack, I slipped it on.

Climbing back up onto the window ledge, I scooted around on my bottom until my feet dangled over the balcony. What if I missed the balcony? It was a long way down to the ground. What if a strong gust of wind took me over?

In the experiment on velocity that we did at Luther, we proved the weight of a falling object increased in proportion to the speed and distance it fell. If I got heavier, I hoped Winnie would be right under me when I hit the ground.

I jumped.

# Seventeen

I skinned my knee, but I didn't care. I wasn't hurt, just scared. I didn't dare look down. Losing my nerve could be fatal. The sidewalk was six floors below. I told myself that it would feel good to be free. Carefully, I began to climb over the wall and onto the living-room balcony. If I slipped, I'd go right off the balcony. My heart banged. I had never been so scared in my life. But I did it.

Safe on the other side, I could see through the glass doors that the living room was empty. Quietly, I slid open the door. I sneaked through the room and out the front door. My knees were knocking together like crazy. But I didn't care. I ran swiftly downstairs to the lobby. Freedom!

Outside, warm air hit me. It felt good. A bus was just pulling up to the stop, so I ran for it. As I paid my fare, I wondered what

Amy would say when she found me gone. What would Eric do? Sinking into an empty seat, I told myself this was no time for sentiment. I was going home!

By the time I reached Tarzana, it was dark. But I didn't care. I was home. I sprang off the bus and walked up the street to my house. There were no street lights, but luckily there was a full moon.

My house looked strange in the dark. The cypress trees lining the front yard seemed menacing as they whispered in the warm wind. How silly I was being! I'd grown up with those trees! But it had never felt creepy walking up the driveway before. I took a deep breath. This was stupid. I was home. There was nothing to be afraid of. I had done this a million times before.

But I had never done it alone in the dark.

At the front door, I took out my key. My hands shook as I searched for the lock. Feeling like a blind person, I traced the keyhole with trembling fingers. I aimed the key into the opening, but the stupid thing wouldn't go in.

"Go in, darn you!" I muttered fiercely. I twisted it around and tried again. This was crazy. The dumb thing didn't fit!

My stomach felt like water. Why wouldn't the key fit? I tried again, but I had no luck.

What was going on?

Something squeaked behind me, and I spun around in fear. This was awful.

A tall white thing swung from the grass. What was it? A ghost? I willed myself to look again. It was not a ghost. In the moonlight, a white wooden sign, staked in the grass, creaked.

Why was there a sign here? I ran over to it. There was no mistaking the foot-high red letters.

"No!"

I screamed again as I read: FOR SALE

So, they'd done it already. Dad said he'd put the house up for sale, but I thought he meant when they got back. My house, my home, was for sale. I'd never live here again. My key would never fit the door again.

Panicked, I ran to the door and kicked it. "I want to come in! I want to come in!" I shouted.

But nothing happened.

I ran around to the back of the house and tried the windows. They wouldn't budge. Not even the side door would open. There was no way in. For the first time in my life, I was locked out.

Sobbing, I rattled the door handle. This was a nightmare. "It's not fair! It's not fair!" I yelled. But it was no use. This was not my home anymore. Slumping down on the porch, I cried even harder.

After a long time, I lifted up my face. The shadowy yard, spooky in the moonlight, did not help. From my tree house hung a stray balloon, empty of air. It was a relic of that other awful moment of my life, Dad's wedding day. It looked pathetic.

Spurred on by anger, I ran to it and ripped it down. I pulled at the yellow ribbon that was still pinned to the trunk.

"You're my tree house—mine, mine, mine!" I screamed. Encircling the trunk with my arms, I cried against the rough bark. When I was done, I took my flute and climbed up the branches.

The patio lights from next door lighted up my tree house. On the floor was a dirty glass and some crumpled music. How long was it since I'd been here? It had probably just been a few weeks. It felt like a lifetime. I would never get back that old life.

I pulled my graduation music from my backpack. I hadn't played it since that night I'd seen Amy sitting on Dad's shoulders. My problems now seemed much bigger than that.

I put the flute to my lips and blew. The notes filtered into the night air. My mind drifted through the soft, blended sounds. Gradually, the music seemed to make sense of the jumble. I'd been so angry last time I'd played this piece. Now it calmed me. As usual, my flute comforted me. The music had a pattern, while my whole life was a jumble. But as I went on playing, the jumble cleared.

Treating Dad and Marcie separately hadn't worked. They wanted to share their lives. They wanted it so bad that they'd forced Amy and me to share, too. Nothing I did would change Dad's being married to Marcie. I knew that now for sure. Maybe I'd always known it, but from this moment, I was going to stop fighting it. I didn't like it any more than I ever had, but fighting only made it worse. My playing got stronger. I would make the best of things. As the music reached a crescendo, I felt determined. I might not fight, but I wasn't going to be a wimp. I'd show Marcie and Winnie that I'm not a kid. Everybody in a family has a right to speak.

If I had to share their lives, then they were going to share mine, too. My non-sharing days were over.

When the police car siren screamed into our driveway, I knew what I had to do. I watched through the branches as two policemen got out of the car.

"Sunday Moon Fairchild? Sunday Moon Fairchild?" called a deep voice.

The policemen shone flashlights on the front of the house. Then they came to the back.

You will not be bossed around, I reminded myself. I stood up. "Here I am!" I called to them in a firm voice.

One of them shone his flashlight up into the branches. "Well, young lady. We are glad to see you," he said. "Wilkins, call the station. We've found our runaway."

"I wasn't a runaway," I corrected him. "I thought this was my home." I sighed as I climbed down from the tree house. "I made a mistake."

The policeman smiled at me. "A lot of people have been worried about you, Miss Fairchild."

He led me to the waiting squad car.

"My name's Officer Jefferson," he offered as he helped me into his car. "But you can call me Officer Jeff." He turned out to be really nice.

On the way to Marcie's, he told me, "I like happily ending stories. Police work usually ends up with someone upset."

"I'm not sure this won't," I told him as the city lights drew closer.

He grinned. "Now, don't you worry. When your grandma sees you, she will be so happy. She sounded very upset..."

"She's not my grandmother."

"Well, she cares about you just the same. And what about that baby sister that you've been telling me about?"

"She'll be glad I'm back," I told him. I knew that for sure.

Amy was glad to see me. I thought I'd be squeezed to death from her little arms around my neck. I guess I hugged her pretty hard, too.

When I pulled away, I saw Winnie standing over me with a chalky face. She looked terrible.

"She gave you a nasty scare, did she?" inquired Officer Jeff.

"I'll say," answered Winnie, folding her arms.

I looked at Winnie and Officer Jeff. I'd show them that I'm not a kid. "I—I'm sorry I scared you, Winnie."

Winnie pushed back her hat. "You certainly did scare me."

"I didn't mean to. I just hated being shut in."

She shook her head. "What else could I do?"

"My dad never shut me in anywhere," I told

her softly, but firmly. "He talks things through with me. He says I'm not stupid."

"It was pretty dumb to run away," Winnie countered.

"I know that," I answered quickly. "But I came back."

Winnie sighed. "I'm glad you did," she said.

"I am, too," piped Amy, and Officer Jeff chuckled.

I didn't speak. But the strange thing was that I think I was glad I came back, too.

# Eighteen

The big day had finally come. Dad and Marcie were coming home. I was excited, but nervous, too. Would Dad be different? Would he think I'd changed? So much had happened to me this past month. I felt so different.

How would it be with Marcie? I didn't think we'd ever be good friends, but we'd have to try to get along. What if I was the only one trying?

As I was thinking about this, the doorbell rang. It was Eric.

"You look great," he complimented me. "I love your shirt. I wish I could come with you."

"I do, too," I told him. "But this is something I have to do alone."

"Right." He touched my nose with' his fingertip. "Come down when you get back."

I still got goosebumps when he touched me. "Okay."

Then he leaned forward and kissed the place he'd touched.

I admit nose-kissing is no big deal, but to me it was wonderful. I probably would have passed out with joy if the phone hadn't rung right then.

Eric gave me a shy smile. "I'll see you later."

"Okay. Bye."

I ran to the phone, bubbling with happiness

It was Julie.

"Hi. Is that you, Sunday?"

"Hi," I said.

"Good luck today."

"Thanks." I gave a little squeal. "I'm so excited. I can't wait to see my dad. And Eric just kissed my nose."

Julie giggled. "Success at last! Listen, say hi to your dad for me."

"Okay."

Julie dropped her voice to a whisper. "Er, Sunday? Carl wants to talk to you."

"Carl?" *Uh-oh.*

"Don't tell him about the four of us, okay?"

"Okay."

There was a silence, and then Carl picked up the receiver. He cleared his throat. "Hi."

I acted like it was normal for him to speak to me. "Hi."

"I hope your dad had a good trip."

"Thank you. But he's not back yet."

"Oh." There was an embarrassed silence. "Well, have a nice day."

He was gone.

The Ninth Wonder of the World— Carl Essentia had been polite.

"That was amazing," I told Julie when she came back on the line. "I've never heard him talk like that before."

"I told him how you said that he should be nicer," she confided.

Winnie bustled into the hall, looking flustered.

"Get off the phone!" she ordered. "We'll be late."

"Okay. Julie, I have to go."

"Okay. Call me later," she said, hanging up.

Amy came out of our room, carrying Ollie, who was dressed in his best clothes.

"Mommy's coming home," she told him.

I guess it hadn't been easy on Amy being away from her mommy. When you're four, you have even fewer choices than when you're 14.

I looked at Amy, Winnie, and me. Dad and Marcie would have no trouble picking us out from the crowd. Winnie was wearing her red polka dots and her wedding cake hat. Amy and I wore white shorts and our "Welcome to L.A." T-shirts.

It was a good thing that I had gotten the medium size instead of the small. I noticed this morning that I was growing out of my Tiny Teen Bra. Change is growth, as Dad would say.

I was thinking of Dad's favorite phrase as I saw him walk off the ship. He looked tan and handsome, loaded down with a huge stuffed bear, a guitar, and two bags.

"Daddy, Daddy, Daddy!" I ran up to him and held him tight. I have never felt so good in my entire life.

We were together again.

"Sunday, my Sunday."

"Daddy, I'm so glad you're back. Did you have a good time?"

"It was wonderful. But I'm glad to be back, too."

Marcie hugged Amy, laughing and crying. "Amy! Amy!"

Amy had one arm around Marcie's neck and was squeezing Dad's leg with the other.

Daddy bent down to her.

"Amy, honey. Give me a kiss."

Marcie's eyes met mine over their heads. *This is it.*

"Hi, Marcie," I said quietly. "I—I hope you

had a good honeymoon."

She looked at me uncertainly. "Well, thank you. Was it okay here?"

Before I could answer, Winnie staggered up breathless, with her hat slipping down over one eye. Her red polka dots jiggled as she moved. "I'm glad you're back!" she bellowed. "It's been a circus at home."

I hid a smile. She didn't remind me of a circus clown anymore, but she still made me laugh.

I put my arm around Amy.

"Ollie's glad you're back, too," I told them. "Right, Amy?"

## About the Author

JANA NOVOTNY HUNTER was born in Czechoslavkia, but moved to London when she was a baby. Today, Jana divides her time between two continents. With her son, Christopher, and her husband, Richard Hunter, Jana lives part of the time in Los Angeles, California and part of it in a small village in the English countryside. Jana has been writing for young people since 1982 and, in 1987, she was awarded the Judy Blume "works in progress" award for a book about a deaf girl.

Jana's special love for young people grows out of her experiences as a textile artist and a teacher. "Young people are great," she says. "As a textile artist, I loved designing their clothes. As a teacher, I loved talking with them. Now, as a writer, I love writing about their special world."

"It's exciting growing up today, but it can be painful sometimes. In my stories, I try to capture the spirit of young people. I write about their dreams and disasters, trials and confusion. But more than anything, I write about their triumphs. Overcoming obstacles is what young people do best."